RV

DanaSullivan

A Chance Wild Apple

BY MARIAN POTTER

Blatherskite
The Shared Room

A Chance Wild Apple

BY MARIAN POTTER

William Morrow and Company

New York   1982

Printed in the United States of America.

  2   3   4   5   6   7   8   9   10

Library of Congress Cataloging in Publication Data

Potter, Marian.
   A chance wild apple.

   Summary: On a Missouri farm in the midst of the Depression, eleven-year-old Maureen has a bit of good luck when she finds a special wild apple tree.
   [1. Farm life—Fiction.   2. Missouri—Fiction.   3. Apple—Fiction]   I. Title.
PZ7.P853Ch   [Fic]   81-18711
ISBN 0-688-01075-X   AACR2

A
Chance
Wild Apple

1.

Maureen McCracken swung on the yard gate at the Wiley place, where she and her family had worked all week. She considered making the house fit for human habitation a privilege, especially since Uncle Millard, Aunt Cora, and their nine children were going to be the inhabitants. The very next day they were going to leave Saint Louis and come to Dotzero, Missouri, to live at the Wiley place, which adjoined the McCracken farm.

All the McCrackens were glad that finally they could do something about Uncle Millard besides worry. He had been laid off his factory job months ago. Aunt Cora hadn't been called back to trim hats at the hat factory since early spring, and it was now August, 1937. Maureen knew that the Depression was so bad that she had to spell it with a capital *D* when she wrote it at school. Uncle Millard couldn't pay the high city rent, and he couldn't make a garden or keep laying hens in the city either.

Mrs. Wiley was making the move to Dotzero possible. She owned so many tracts of land between Dotzero and Beaumont, where she lived alone in a brick house, that people said she was land poor from paying taxes. Of all her acres, the Wiley place meant most to her, for it had belonged to her dead husband's family. She didn't want the house to fall down. When she had learned of Uncle Millard's needs, she let him know his family could live there rent free in exchange for doing a few odd jobs around the place.

Maureen wondered what made a job odd. Maybe fixing the self-closing gate was an example. If so, she and her little brother, Walter, had already done that one for Uncle Millard. They had renailed the gate chain so that the weight of the piece of scrap iron hung on it closed the gate with a firm thump.

Maureen intended to continue to be a source of help, inspiration, and information to her cousins coming out from the city. She looked down the hill, across the narrow valley of Lost Creek to the bordering highlands. Very likely Uncle Millard's family didn't know that Dotzero was in the Saint Francois Mountains. Maureen herself hadn't realized it until she had seen the name printed on her fifth-grade geography map just southwest of Saint Louis. She felt she had discovered the Saint Francois Mountains and was glad the rough, hilly land had a name.

She could see the railroad right-of-way in Lost Creek valley but not Dotzero depot, which was more than a

8

mile down the Missouri Pacific track. Dad had told Maureen how Dotzero got its name, but she doubted that Uncle Millard had told his kids. Maureen didn't want them to think Dotzero was an unimportant place. She'd tell them right away how the railroad survey started there. Surveyors had put a decimal point and a zero down on their chart as the starting point. When the railroad was finished, the first station was named for the mark on the map—Dotzero.

The Wiley place had low fields in the creek valley and high pastures on the ridge. Maureen wasn't sure she could show her cousins its exact boundaries, except where it joined McCracken land. Their hayfield was close to the Wiley house.

Maureen was sure Uncle Millard's family would be pleased with the Wiley house, although its paint was weathered and much of its fancy wood trim gone. The house roof extended over the front porch, and the windows of the small upstairs rooms were tucked in the gables. The house had a low, cozy look that Maureen liked.

Walter, followed by Tisket, McCrackens' fox terrier, came around the side of the house. Walter was eight, but he was still baby soft and plump as a new pillow. "I think it's almost suppertime, Maureen. When are we going home?" he asked.

"I'm ready and waiting. Everything is done inside. I guess we'll go as soon as Mit cuts the weeds." She pointed to the far corner of the yard where Mit, their older brother, swung a heavy scythe.

Maureen broke off clusters of blue ironweed and plumes

of goldenrod. "See here, Walter, yellow and blue go together. That's because yellow and blue make green. I know because I scribbled blue Crayola over yellow, and sure enough—green."

"Why?" Walter asked.

"Why? Just does, that's all." She broke another stem. "Why did this weed patch turn into a regular flower bed?"

The swish of the mowing blade came closer. "Look out, you kids, I'm coming through," Mit warned.

Maureen and Walter stamped down stalks getting out of the way. Mit stopped to wipe sweat from his face on the shoulder of his shirt. The long, sharp blade flashed in the sun as he brandished the scythe. "Want to try this, Maureen?"

She shook her head. "Not now. We've got to put these in water and leave them here for Uncle Millard." She wouldn't let Mit make a fool of her. They both knew she couldn't handle that tall, crooked-handled scythe. She pointed to the weedy flowers. "You could leave a few."

"No, I'm cutting them all. This yard is such a ragged mess. It looks like a sheep's rear end."

"You just better watch out how you talk, Milton McCracken," Maureen warned, although she knew he wouldn't pay attention to her. At one time, she and Mit had been near the same size, and she could pin him in a wrestling match. Now, at fourteen, he was heavier and stronger. He had graduated from eighth grade, was finished with school, and thought he knew everything. Maureen watched him mow. When he did a man's work, he seemed more than ever like Dad. Of course, Dad didn't

10

take a comb out of his back pocket and run it through his hair every ten minutes the way Mit did.

"Mit could save himself work." Maureen swung her bouquet. "We'd wear this yard bare in no time, playing games when we come visiting. There's bound to be a cousin your age, Walter. I know Crystal is eleven, same as I am. I can't wait until they come. . . . Yippee, yippee," Maureen suddenly shrieked with joy.

Walter tried to keep up with her long-legged leaps to the cistern. She filled the drinking glass that was kept there with water and stuck in the flowers.

Maureen was careful not to slosh water on the new linoleum as she carried the bouquet to the table in the Wiley house kitchen.

In the adjoining room, she inhaled the clean smell of flour paste drying under new wallpaper. There wasn't a single place to show how Mama had struggled to match the pattern of roses and cover the cracked plaster on the crooked walls.

Footsteps clumped, and the door to the enclosed stairway swung into the room. A rocking chair was pushed out. Then Dad appeared, carrying a straight chair.

Maureen slid into the rocker. The twisted wire that braced it squeaked as she rocked. "Aunt Cora will like this."

Dad sat on the straight chair, and Walter leaned against his knees. "We found a few more sticks of furniture back under the eaves. There's an old set of springs and mattress up there that look like they died of the palsy, but they'll have to do for the present."

11

Maureen studied Dad's face to make sure he wasn't getting discouraged. His forehead was fair, his cheeks and neck deeply tanned, because he always wore a peaked denim cap when he worked on the railroad extra gang. There were wrinkles in his white forehead but no black looks from his gray eyes.

Mama came down the stairway, her arms full of old books and magazines. There were cobwebs in her wavy brown hair, and her cotton dress was damp with sweat.

"Give your mother that rocker," Dad said.

When Maureen moved to the floor, Mama sank into the rocker and fanned herself with a magazine. "It's hotter than blue blazes in the crawl space over the kitchen. I dragged these out of there." She picked up one of the books and turned the pages. "Old books of the Wiley family. I thought I might as well bring them down. Millard's gang might need something for entertainment here in the country."

Maureen got up and held the back of the rocker as she jumped up and down. "I can't wait until tomorrow."

"Simmer down, Maureen. It's not going to be all peaches and cream," Mama cautioned.

"Could be. We've got ripe peaches, and Molly's cream is the best."

Dad looked around the room. "I don't know about peaches, but I'd say we have this place in apple-pie order."

"Clean, anyhow," Mama said with satisfaction. "And enough furniture for light housekeeping, which is Cora's style."

12

Maureen pulled two frames from beneath the stack of magazines. One was a mirror dim with grime. She wiped the glass of the other on the hem of her dress. "This looks sorta like Lost Creek. Did somebody take a picture and color it?"

Dad studied the watercolor landscape. "I'd say it's a hand-painted picture. Dotzero State Forest, in back of us. One of the Wileys painted this. Some of them were talented."

Maureen handled the frames carefully. "I'll clean them and put them up. Plenty of nails in the walls. Walter, get me that cleaning rag on the porch."

Maureen hung the cleaned mirror on the kitchen wall and studied her reflection. She tried to push some waves into her straight black hair. Then she tilted her head in various poses, hoping for an appealing look.

"Why are you grinning at yourself?" Walter asked.

"Smiling," Maureen corrected. She straightened her shoulders without anyone telling her to do so. She was growing taller, and it was easy to slump.

After they had admired the watercolor picture hung on the wall of roses, Walter said he could tell without a clock that it was suppertime.

Dad glanced out the window. "Mit's finished his job, so we'd better hike home and do chores. We have to leave some odd jobs for Millard. Mrs. Wiley expects him to nail down a loose board or two." They went into the kitchen, where he noticed the bouquet. "Maureen, that's the finishing touch."

13

Mama walked across the kitchen on her toes so the tacks on her shoe heels wouldn't wear the linoleum. Carefully she closed the back door.

At the gate Maureen waited for Mit. "How do you like the way we fixed this so it would close?"

"S'all right." Mit leaned the scythe against the fence, picked up a stone, and threw it at a chipmunk. He sure could peg a rock just where he wanted it.

"You did a lot to help," Maureen said, hoping for return praise of her work.

"It's nothing to what I'm going to do. Something that will make a world of difference for us."

"Like what?"

"Just never you mind, Maureen. You'll know when the time comes." Mit tried to see how far he could spit. He seemed to think spitting made him manly.

During the evening, Maureen had so much to think of that she didn't wonder about Mit's plan. Although she was tired from all her work at the Wiley place, she had trouble falling asleep that night. It was like trying to doze off on Christmas Eve, with the added hindrance of stifling heat in her small room at the stop of the stairs. Twice she woke Mama and Dad when she turned on the flashlight in their room to look at the clock.

2.

Next morning Mama assigned Maureen plenty of jobs. Still, the day dragged until evening when all the McCrackens walked the mile and a half to Dotzero depot to meet Number 41.

Maureen wished someone besides the station agent, who had to meet the train, had been at the depot to see all her kinfolks arrive. She watched the tall signal beside the track and saw the semaphore drop to show a red light in the evening dusk. Far off a locomotive whistle moaned, and finally the headlight of the engine shone down the track.

Trains didn't stop long at Dotzero. Passengers had to be ready to hop right off. Uncle Millard, carrying a sleeping child and two shopping bags, came down the coach steps.

Children lugging bags and boxes followed him. Aunt Cora was last, dragging a bulging suitcase tied with rope.

As the train pulled out, Uncle Millard's family clustered around him. He put down his shopping bags. "Here we are, bag and baggage, the whole kit and kaboodle. We didn't leave anybody on the train, did we? Here, Yvonne, go to your mama." He handed the little girl, now awake and fretting, to Aunt Cora.

Mama hugged Uncle Millard because he was her own brother. Dad pumped his hand. Uncle Millard was special for Maureen, too, because folks often said she was an O'Neil, same as Uncle Millard, Grandma, and Mama.

Even without burdens, Uncle Millard didn't stand straight. One shoulder was higher than the other from his years of work at the factory bench. He was bareheaded, and all his face was pale as Dad's forehead. Maureen put her arms around his waist. "You've got everybody. I counted. All nine kids," Maureen shouted. The noisy machines of Uncle Millard's factory had made him partly deaf.

Mama took Yvonne from Aunt Cora, who smiled, showing the gap from a missing front tooth. With hands free, she tried to anchor the knot of red hair that was slipping from the top of her head. Her hairdo seemed about to fall apart, like the suitcase that Mit had taken from her.

Maureen had not seen her cousins for more than a year. She'd be a while sorting them out. "Here, I'll carry that," she offered, and took a bulky package from a blond-haired girl smaller than herself. "Are you Crystal?"

"Crystal. That sounds funny. Hardly anyone calls me that. I'm Skeets."

Mama jiggled Yvonne. "You don't have a baby anymore, Cora. All your kids have grown so."

"Everybody but Skeets. She's stayed a half-pint. Little but all there," Aunt Cora said, as if she was especially pleased with Skeets. "My! Maureen has shot up. So big for her age."

Maureen let her shoulders droop so she wouldn't seem so tall.

"We'd better take you folks to the Wiley place while there's still daylight. Only one way to get there. Shank's mare." Dad started walking.

Maureen ran ahead. Then, in order to see everyone, she turned and walked backward with her bundle bumping against her legs.

"Watch out, Maureen, you'll fall," Mama cautioned.

"Won't either," Maureen disputed. "I know this road so well I could walk it blindfolded. I know the McCracken place, shortcuts to the Wiley place, everything around here in the Saint Francois Mountains.

"We've got the Wiley house fixed up for you, and it was some job too. Want to know what we've done?" Maureen didn't wait for an answer. "Walter and I were put in charge of one room. We swept two dead birds, a bushel of leaves, and some other junk out of there. Well, no wonder, with two windowlights broken. They're fixed now. Mit puttied them in. That was a lot easier than one of his jobs when he was. . . ."

17

"Pipe down, Maureen," Mit said, as he caught up with her. "You don't have to tell everything you know right away."

"Sure, but I'll finish." She raised her voice so all could hear. "Mit propped up the privy, and he almost—" Suddenly Maureen was flat on her back. She felt silly and jumped up quickly. She wasn't sure that Mit had tripped her, but there was no other reason for stumbling.

She fell into step beside Skeets. "Wasn't it fun to ride on the train?"

"Kinda. It stopped at a lot of little towns," Skeets said. "None as little as Dotzero, though. The train stayed a long time at Beaumont, where my grandma lives."

"*Your* grandma?" Maureen questioned. "Well, I guess that's right." Still, Maureen thought, she was much closer to Grandma than her cousins, who seldom saw her.

"How much farther is it?" Skeets asked.

"Just a hop, skip, and a jump." Maureen bounded ahead to demonstrate.

"Careful there, Maureen. You'll take another header," Dad warned.

No one said a word to Skeets when she ran far ahead. With her bulky package, Maureen knew she couldn't keep up with Skeets. Anyhow, she wanted to hear what Mama was telling Aunt Cora about the Wiley house.

"Dad cleaned out the cistern, Aunt Cora," Maureen interrupted. "We didn't want you to get typhoid fever. We cleaned the gutters, too, and tarred holes in the tin roof. Just about the most fun we had was getting the woodchucks out from under the house. Foundation stones were loose, and woodchucks made burrows under there. Tisket almost went crazy when she found them."

Aunt Cora looked at the evening sky. "Soon be night. I'd like to see what I'm moving into before it gets pitch-dark. I almost forgot how dark it gets in the sticks. Don't dawdle, kids. There's no street light in Dotzero."

"But there is Dotzero school and Stackhouse store and the post office. The post office is in the store," Maureen explained. "You saw the depot, and—"

"Millard and Cora grew up around here the same as the rest of us, Maureen. You folks will have to excuse her for telling you things you already know," Mama apologized. "She's wound up tighter than a toy on Christmas morning."

"One thing they don't know, Mama, is that they have a new linoleum because you said not even a good house-keeper could keep that rough floor clean. It's awful pretty, blue with yellow teapots. Sears economy grade. That's the cheapest. You know you said if I got to hankering for any-thing taking cash, I could forget it because all our cash went for the linoleum and—"

Mama patted Maureen's shoulder. "These folks are tired after packing up and getting down here. Some of your report can wait."

Maureen saw no need for waiting. The little children were lagging behind. Aunt Cora was concerned about the dark. Uncle Millard was burdened with luggage. Maybe he was like Dad and got out of heart. If so, he and all his family would be off to a bad start. Maureen felt she should point out some of their advantages.

"You're lucky you can move into the Wiley place," she

said. "Mrs. Wiley tries to collect cash rent from all her other places. She has a lot of them. Some people claim she's stingy and will give you everything the hen lays except the egg, but I think—"

"Maureen!" Mama exclaimed. "Now that's enough out of you. You're just rattling on, showing off."

The scolding embarrassed Maureen. She was thankful that Skeets, who had sat down beside the road to wait, was too far ahead to hear it. When they reached her, Dad handed Maureen another heavy bag to carry.

Dad squatted down with his back to Skeets. "What's the matter? Do you need a lift? Hop on." Skeets put her arms around Dad's neck, and he hoisted her up on his back.

Maureen could hardly believe what she was seeing. Skeets was way too old to be carried piggyback. Maureen was furious. If her own dad wanted to carry anyone, he could carry her, even if her feet would almost drag on the ground.

All at once she was exhausted. For days she'd helped get the Wiley place ready. The night before she'd been awake most of the time. She'd been loaded down with junk. She felt as if she had just strength enough to do one more thing—pull Skeets right off Dad's back.

3

Maureen had expected days of play to start at the Wiley place immediately, but she was home alone watching the cold-pack canner. Mama had said Maureen's being so dependable gave her time to help Millard's family get settled. Mit, Walter, and even Tisket had gone to the Wiley place with Mama again.

Being dependable had drawbacks. For hours, Maureen had kept the boiling water at the right level around the jars of green beans, but still the time hadn't come to turn out the kerosene burner under the big pot. At least, she could escape from the hot kitchen occasionally to the tire swing in the oak tree of the front yard.

Maureen pulled back the tire and braced her toes to give herself a push. At the foot of the hill below the McCracken house, Lost Creek curved around their bottom field, which was infested with tall, rank Johnson grass. She twisted the swing rope and faced the opposite direction to see if anyone was coming home on the path through their uncut hayfield. The field was hazy with heat, and no one was in sight.

She considered ringing the farm bell that hung on the side of the apple-packing shed. That would bring them running. But the bell was for emergencies. Mama might think she'd been scalded by a jar of exploding beans. Loneliness wasn't exactly an emergency.

As she swung, she admired the three dormer windows of the McCracken house. She thought they gave it great style. She also liked the wide gambrel roof of the barn. But the hayloft was empty, and the roof seemed like spreading arms with nothing to hug.

McCrackens had no mules now, and without them Dad and Mit had been unable to raise corn or to make hay to winter Molly, their milk cow. Hard luck, not hard times, had taken the mules. During a cloudburst, Mit had driven the team into a washed-out ford on Lost Creek. McCrackens seldom spoke of the loss, for Mit had taken it hard. Besides, they all knew that more than the mules could have drowned.

Molly's steep pasture adjoining the barn lot blended into McCrackens' woods. Maureen knew where a sagging wire fence separated McCrackens' woods from Dotzero State Forest, which stretched to the top of the ridge and far beyond. A tiny building showed above the highest treetop. That box was the lookout of the state forest fire tower.

The whistle of Number 32 for Dotzero crossing told

her the time had finally come to turn off the stove. She watched the train cross the trestle, then hurried inside to take the quart jars, one by one, from the steaming water with the jar lifter. She made sure each jar lid was tightly sealed before she went back outside. Tisket came panting across the yard. Then Maureen heard the welcome murmur of voices and saw Walter and Mama coming.

"Walter and I want to go swimming, Mama," Maureen called in greeting. "He's all red in the face. See how hot he is? So am I. My dress is sticking to me. The beans are all done and cooling, no jars cracked. Can we go? Can we?"

Mama sat down in a porch chair and took off her broad-brimmed straw hat. The heat curled her hair into damp ringlets around her face. With her foot, she pushed at Tisket, who panted and snapped at gnats. "Get away, Tisket. You make me feel hotter."

"Well, can we, Mama?" Maureen implored.

"I don't blame you for wanting to jump in the creek, Maureen. But you know the rules. You can't go without someone else along who can swim, and that's not Walter."

Mama couldn't swim and didn't understand that a person who could was able to keep from drowning in deep water. Maureen handed her a dipper of water from the bucket on the porch bench. "Where's Mit? He could go with us."

"He stayed at Millard's, hoping Mrs. Wiley will come by so he can devil her again for work. . . . They burn two lamps over there all night while the kids are getting used to things. So we need coal oil, and we haven't asked for mail for a week. You better run down to the store."

Mama made a mile-and-a-half walk in the heat to the store sound like running across the yard to the packing shed. "I'll go, but I won't run, and Walter has to come with me. I need company. Get the oil can, Walter," she directed.

Instead of taking their shortcut path, Maureen and Walter started down the lane so they could pick up apples at the edge of the orchard, which was on the slope back of the barn. Walter looked rounder than usual after Maureen filled his pockets with Early Harvest windfalls.

"What games did you play at Uncle Millard's?" she asked.

Walter didn't reply. His lips were puckered, and he had a look of deep concentration on his face. A faint note came from his lips.

"Walter! You can whistle. I knew you'd get the hang of it if you kept trying." Walter blew the same note twice more. "That's it. Your problem is that your cheeks are kind of fat to wave the way they must to whistle."

Walter allowed his lips to spread into a smile. "Skeets taught me," he said, and then puckered his lips to resume practice.

"She didn't do any such thing. Nobody can teach you. All at once, there you are, whistling."

"No, she told me to make a hole in my face and push, so I did. I'm going to whistle tunes the way Dad does when he's happy."

Walter wasn't much company on the long walk. He couldn't chat and whistle his one note at the same time.

Besides the store and post office, the Stackhouses had farmland. Maureen and Walter were passing the Stackhouse pasture when they saw livestock ahead on the road. The jackasses and jennet asses were as big as mules. They laid back their long ears and moved aside when Maureen picked up a stick and waved it at them. "This year, anyway, we don't have to worry about those old jacks and jennies breaking our fences and trampling our corn, since we don't have any."

With a stiff, jerky gait, an old sorrel mare stumbled out of the roadside brush. Her back was swayed from the burden of years. "Why, there's Mr. Stackhouse's Patsy. She's not supposed to be out of her pasture on free range." Maureen noticed an open farm gate. "Give me an apple, Walter. Maybe we can coax her back where she belongs." Maureen held out the apple and called, "Cope, cope, Patsy, cope."

Patsy breathed heavily as she followed Maureen into the pasture. Her sorrel hide was salted with gray, and her muzzle was hoary. With loose lips, she took the apple from the palm of Maureen's hand.

Carefully Maureen pushed the plank latch to close the gate behind them as she and Walter left the pasture. "You have to keep your fingers down when you give a horse an apple," she explained, "or you might lose one. Of course, Patsy might not have much in the way of teeth. She's so old."

"How old?" Walter asked.

"Nobody knows except Sterling Price Stackhouse, and

maybe Mrs. Stackhouse. They don't use her. Do you want to know why they keep her?" Maureen asked, as if struck with an interesting thought.

Walter whistled a note in reply.

"Well, they keep her because once she had this special little colt. It was a unicorn. I saw it myself in this pasture right after it was born. It was a long time ago, when you were too small to walk to the store with me. It was stretched out in the sun; I thought it was dead. Patsy is so gentle I went close to see for sure. It was alive all right and got up on its wobbly legs and looked at me. That was really spooky, Walter. Its eyes were like a person's eyes, not a colt's. Its hoofs were red as strawberries. I reached out and touched the top of its head between the ears. Then I felt a little stub of a horn, and I jumped. I knew for sure it was a unicorn."

Walter stopped whistling. "How do you know so much about unicorns?"

"First I heard of them was in a Mother Goose book," Maureen explained, as they walked on toward the store. "There was this rhyme about a lion and a unicorn having a fight over a crown."

"Who won?"

"Doesn't matter, Walter. Every now and then I read about a unicorn. It tells about one in Psalms, right in the middle of the Bible. So you know it's true."

"I never saw one. Maybe you didn't, either." Walter took a bite from an apple.

"They're not easy to see. I was flabbergasted to find one here in Dotzero."

26

Walter smacked his lips. "What did Stackhouses do with their unicorn?"

"A unicorn isn't like a horse or a mule. You can't train it for the saddle or to pull a buggy or to plow corn. Stackhouses didn't let on they had it. I guess they just kept it for a while as a curiosity."

"Where is it now? I want to see it." Walter tossed away his apple core as if ready to start.

"I wish I could tell you, but I don't know. Now when we go into the store, don't say anything to Mrs. Stackhouse about that unicorn. Let me do the talking."

Even in summer, with the door open, the store smelled of tobacco, soap, leather shoes, and rubber boots. Maureen and Walter went to the postal window. That corner of the store smelled of mucilage and dusty mailbags.

Mrs. Stackhouse seemed to be suspended in front of the grocery counter. She was so fat that the low stool she sat on didn't show; she was so short that her legs dangled. "I'll save myself a trip over there, Maureen. I know there is no mail for McCracken."

"Any mail for O'Neil, our Uncle Millard?" Maureen inquired.

"A little girl asked for their mail this morning. She said I should call her Skeets. Such a friendly little thing. Long, yellow hair. Just as cute as a button."

Maureen didn't want to talk of Skeets's charms, so she changed the subject. "Old Patsy was out on the road, but I got her closed up again."

"Much obliged, Maureen. Somebody cut through the pasture and left the gate open again. It must be half a dozen times this spring and summer Patsy's been loose. I'd hate for her to be hit by a car. She shouldn't be out on free range. Mrs. Wiley takes advantage of free range, and we could do without those old jacks and jennies crashing around here night and day. But as long as there is free range, or free anything, she'll get in on it. I was dumbfounded that she let Millard move into the Wiley place rent free. Has she put him to work yet?"

"Oh, yes, he's doing odd jobs." Maureen crossed to the grocery side of the store and handed Mrs. Stackhouse the kerosene can.

She lowered her feet to the floor. "Out of oil again? It takes a lot when you use an oil stove for canning. Likely your mom is filling jars for Millard's outfit, too. They'll have a hard row to hoe, coming this time of year. What does your mom think of Cora's housekeeping?"

"She said not even a demon housekeeper could keep up with nine kids."

"I've lost count of all those children. The oldest is a girl. What's her name?" Mrs. Stackhouse asked.

"Vido. Her real name is Viola, but the little kids couldn't say it," Maureen reported.

"I feel for Vido." Mrs. Stackhouse clicked her tongue. "I imagine Cora puts all the work on that girl."

"Then Drucilla. That's Dessie. She was fourteen in April." Maureen liked to list names and ages. "She's finished eighth grade, but she'll come to school here to review. She says there's not much else to do in Dotzero. Then there's Oren, their first boy. That's all he needed to be to make him special."

"And Skeets. She taught me to whistle." Walter blew a note as proof.

"Her name is Crystal. Fragile, handle with care, like your rubber stamp." Maureen pointed to the post-office corner. "Then there are the twins, Bernard and Buford."

"Boots and Buddy," Walter translated.

"And that just leaves the three least ones. Myrtle, that's Mertie. She's seven. Conrad. They call him Chigger. He's got red hair like Aunt Cora. And Yvonne. You'd think her name started with *E*, but no. Starts with *Y*."

Mrs. Stackhouse walked behind the counter. "You'll be in often to buy for that gang. It's lucky Cleve McCracken will get some work on the extra gang until winter. They have Oren and you've got Mit, and boys that age can put away groceries." Mrs. Stackhouse unscrewed the cap on the oil can. "We could use a strong young fellow like Mit around here this fall. There's corn to be cut. We'd make it worth Mit's while, and he'd get his dinner free. Ask him to come talk to Sterling."

"Oh, I will. He'll be so tickled because he's been hunting work. Soon as you get my oil, I'll beat it home and tell him."

Maureen intended to do just that, but when they got home supper was ready. Mit was right there, combing his hair at the kitchen mirror, but all Maureen thought of was food.

A bit of salt pork was cooked with the green beans. There was a bowl of sliced, juicy tomatoes and a platter of steaming sweet corn from the garden. Mama's biscuits were hot from the oven.

Mama watched Maureen reach for the butter. "Just move your knife back about an inch toward you. That pound has to last the rest of the week."

"Why? Is Molly going dry already?"

Mama passed the butter without taking any. "Oh, no, but I took this week's second pound over to Millard's. Molly's cream will make enough butter for all of us for a while. Until they get lined up over there."

"How long will that be?" Maureen asked.

"It's not on a schedule, like a railroad timetable," Mama said. "We'll just have to be patient and help when we can."

"Mrs. Wiley is getting her ducks in a row," Dad said. "She gave me a lift when I was coming home from work. In the back of her old Durant, she had a roll of barbed wire for Millard to fix fences. He'll be over directly to borrow our wire stretchers. Mrs. Wiley says that since she's got somebody on the place, she's going to raise beef cattle and have Millard and Oren feed stock this winter."

When supper was over, Maureen scraped the dishes without being told and put table scraps in Tisket's pan. Then she took a towel to dry the dishes Mama washed. "Mrs. Stackhouse wanted to know about Aunt Cora's housekeeping," Maureen said. "And she talked about what a hard time we would all have and how we'd have to buy at the store and how much Mit must eat."

"You didn't need to be talking about me," Mit shouted.

"I wasn't. Then she— Oh, Mit, Mr. Stackhouse wants you to come see him about a job, picking corn."

Mit jumped up. "Now that's important, and you were

30

blabbing other stuff. You sure took your time about telling me."

"Get yourself down there first thing in the morning, Mit." Dad sounded pleased.

"I'm not waiting for morning. I'm going right now." The screen banged behind Mit as he bounded down the porch steps.

Mama looked extra pretty when she smiled. "It does sound promising, and every bit helps."

Walter's bedtime train whistled as it went through on the nearby tracks, but he was allowed to stay up and wait for Mit's news. Walter brought a pencil and paper bag to the kitchen table. Maureen watched him draw a face with a cluster of scribbled curls at the top of the head. "Who's that?" she asked.

"Vido. She's pretty."

Maureen shook her head. "She hardly ever smiles."

Walter made another circle. "When you draw a head, you put the eyes halfway down. Skeets showed me. This is Skeets. She's pretty."

"She is not," Maureen disputed. "She's got a face like a pan of milk."

"Now that's enough, you two. We're not running a beauty contest," Mama reminded them.

Walter began to sketch the McCracken house. Maureen was amazed to see him draw the dormer windows so that they fitted into the roof. She had tried many times but had never been able to make such a drawing. "Walter, you've figured it out! The windows are right."

31

He didn't look up. "Skeets taught me."

"Skeets! What does she know about our house?"

"She was drawing the Wiley house, and I tried to draw our house, so she showed me." Walter added the chimney and heavy smoke.

"Needy like they are, you wouldn't think they'd have paper to waste on scribbling." Maureen sniffed. "She'd better save her pencil tablet for school."

"She wasn't wasting paper," Walter explained. "She drew in the yard dust with a nail."

"So she wasn't any help to Aunt Cora, just messing around in the dirt like that." Maureen grunted. "I don't think she can do any kind of work. Be dependable."

Dad chuckled. "Has the green-eyed monster captured Maureen?"

"Green-eyed monster? What's that?" Maureen asked.

"Jealousy. You have to watch out for it." Mama was smiling too.

Maureen shrugged. "Nothing to be jealous about. I just get tired of Walter's talk. It's Skeets this and Skeets that. It's all I hear, what little I see of him. He's always over there."

Mama had lit the lamp by the time they heard someone coming. Mit hit the porch steps hard enough to knock them loose. He burst into the kitchen. "I start Monday."

Mama got up and threw her arms around him. "That's wonderful. Imagine getting your first job when times are so tough."

Dad patted Mit's shoulder. "Now that's good news."

"You'll be hearing more, too," Mit promised. "I'll save all my money, so you'll have more good news."

Walter hugged Mit around the knees, and Maureen crowded in to tug at his shirtsleeve. "I helped you get work. I told you about it, didn't I?"

"Yeah, finally." Mama and Walter let go of Mit so he could sit down. "I knew Mr. Stackhouse would offer me work."

"I sure wish I could bring in a little something," Maureen said.

"An eleven-year-old girl! Are you kidding?" Mit shook his head in disbelief.

"It's bed for you now, Walter. You've heard the big news," Mama said.

Walter went into the dark hall. "Come up with me, Maureen."

She followed him up the stairs. "I'm glad Mit got work, but he'll be too big for his britches. There will be no living with him, Walter." A bit of light shone through the west window at the top of the stairs. "No need to be scared to come upstairs alone. It's not clear dark."

"I'm not afraid. I wanted you to come tell me again about that little unicorn."

"Oh, sure, Walter." Maureen was pleased that he wanted her to do something for him. Mit didn't need her. He'd soon be off working. Even if Skeets was trying to take Walter away from her, she'd go to Uncle Millard's the very next day and put a stop to it.

4

"I'm putting my own house in order," Mama announced the next morning. "It's Thursday and no wash done yet this week. I'll start it, and you can pick beans, Maureen. Hot as it will be, we'll have to can them this afternoon."

Maureen took a bushel basket with her to the garden, which was handy to the kitchen. She was tall enough to reach the long pods at the top of the green tepees formed by the bean vines. Before long Maureen was tired of the sight of Kentucky Wonder pole beans.

At the sound of whistling, she peered through the vines and saw Walter heading for the Wiley place with Tisket at his heels. Maureen left her basket half full and raced ahead of him across the hayfield.

Usually she jumped over the flattened wire between the field and the brushy Wiley pasture. But Uncle Millard had fixed the fence, and she had to roll carefully under the bottom strand of new barbed wire. Then she waited and held the wire up so Walter wouldn't snag his shirt when he rolled under.

There were no shouts of children playing, but as soon as they came in sight of the house, they knew something was going on at the Wiley place. Mrs. Wiley's Durant sedan was at the gate, and Mrs. Wiley herself stood in the yard reading something to Uncle Millard's assembled family.

Maureen and Walter tried to ease into the group, but she eyed them sharply. "I'm glad you McCrackens showed up so you'll know you've got a purebred neighbor." She waved a document at Uncle Millard, who put his hand back of his ear. She raised her voice. "Millard, I've read you his pedigree, Epitome of Lower Upson, a genuine registered Hereford sire. If I was to tell you what I paid for him, you'd think I was out of my mind. But you can't beat good stock in animals or people. Since you're getting fences mended, I closed my deal on Epitome and had him trucked in. We'll haul in four cows tomorrow and more when I get a reasonable buy. Make sure the pasture gates are closed. These city-born-and-raised children might not know an open gate is worse than an unlocked door." With her sharp, black eyes, Mrs. Wiley stared at Maureen's cousins, one by one. "Epitome of Lower Upson is no animal for free range. I let some of my stock loose to graze down the roadsides, but not this fellow."

She folded the pedigree and put it in her big black pocketbook. Even in summer Mrs. Wiley wore long sleeves. The print design of her cotton dress looked like dried-up berries, and it had no trim at all. Maureen thought her straw hat had once been navy blue and good enough for church. Now it had faded to gray, and the center of the crown poked up like a plant gone to seed.

Mrs. Wiley stood back and surveyed the weather-beaten house. "There's a loose board on the gable needs fixing. My husband is in the Wiley cemetery with the rest of the Wileys. If you want to make a whole cemetery full of people happy, you'll help me keep this place from falling down. I hope you can manage here."

"Don't you worry yourself, Mrs. Wiley." Aunt Cora smiled and showed the gap from her missing tooth. "You let us move in here when we had no where to turn. I've found things work out so. I go by Scripture. Psalms 37:25. 'I have been young and now am old, yet have I not seen the righteous forsaken, nor his seed begging bread.' "

Mrs. Wiley didn't nod in agreement the way most people did when Scripture was quoted. She stared at Aunt Cora with her piercing black eyes. "King David was great for writing songs, and that may have been his experience. I'm not always in agreement with him. Now I must stop at some of my other places on my way home to Beaumont. Keep an eye on Epitome. He's a real aristocrat."

When Mrs. Wiley's car lurched down the rutted lane, Aunt Cora said she was worn out with that woman and would have to lie down for a while. As she went inside, she pointed to the grime around the door facing. "You kids get started scrubbing this off. Use the lye soap your

Aunt Lillian brought over. I saw Mrs. Wiley staring at those fingerprints."

Uncle Millard picked up an ax from beside the house. "I'll see if I can still swing this thing my boss lady brought me. With an aristocrat in the pasture, she wants the sprouts cut."

Since Oren was the oldest boy, Maureen expected him to go along and help Uncle Millard. Instead, he found his place in one of the Wiley books and sat down with his back to a porch post. Aunt Cora had done a good job patching his pants, which were unbuckled at the knees to make them look longer. Oren's hair wasn't trained like Mit's and flopped down as he bent over his book.

"What are you reading?" Maureen asked.

Oren didn't answer. He wasn't deaf like Uncle Millard, but when he read he didn't hear anything around him.

There was plenty of noise and confusion. The little children pushed each other about and shrieked. They didn't have any game in mind. Skeets brought a pail of soapy water. Instead of using it, she tucked her dress into her bloomers and turned cartwheels across the yard.

Vido had a pan of McCracken beans to snap, but she gazed idly down the empty lane. "Sure is hot. Nothing else to think about."

"Nobody walking by, no store windows to look into." Dessie pushed her red hair back of her ears and squinted her little blue eyes, making them even smaller. "There's no park or anything."

"Park? Why do you need a park when you've got the

whole Dotzero State Forest?" Maureen pointed to the dark woods along the ridge above them.

"There's Forest Park in Saint Louis," Dessie said, "and it has ice-cream stands and the monkey house and chimpanzee shows, not just a bunch of trees."

Maureen thought she should point out some interesting facts to her glum cousins. "Trees aren't all alike. There are cedars for Christmas and for fence posts; oak trees for acorns, that's the mast that makes the pigs fat; and hickories and walnuts to make us fat. There's sassafras for spring tea and elms, just for instance."

Dessie shrugged. "Just a lot of green trees."

"Different kinds of green, though," Maureen continued. "Willows by Lost Creek are different from dark green oaks, and trunks are different too. Sycamores are white—" Maureen stopped. No one was listening.

"Got no electricity to plug in the radio," Vido said. "Hard to work without music. I certainly would like to hear 'Wagon Wheels' or 'Stormy Weather' or something."

Skeets completed a cartwheel an inch from the step. "We won't see any more movies."

"Might," Maureen said brightly. "There's a picture show in Beaumont. On Monday nights, it's only ten cents. Tuesday nights you get dishes. Wednesday is bank night, and you might win a pile of money."

"Before Dad got laid off, we went to the movies once at Loews State Theater," Skeets recalled. "It's a palace."

"Palaces are only in fairy tales," Maureen objected.

"It's a palace," Skeets repeated.

There was Walter with his mouth open listening to

38

Skeets. Maureen felt the morning was being wasted. "Come on, let's play some games," she suggested.

"It's too hot," Dessie whined.

"How about rotten egg?" Maureen asked. "That doesn't take much running."

"Rotten egg! I never heard of that stinky game. Whew!" Skeets held her nose and ran across the porch. "How about hit-the-book?" She knocked Oren's book into his face.

He jumped up, grabbed the scrub pail, and threw water at Skeets, who dodged. Dessie got drenched. As she screamed and lunged after Oren, she tramped on Mertie's bare foot and knocked Chigger off the porch to the ground, where he lay yelling. Vido scattered beans from her lap when she ran to pick up Chigger. Aunt Cora appeared at the door and threatened to give everyone a good licking.

Walter tugged at Maureen's arm. "Let's go home."

Maureen thought of the unfilled basket in the garden and of Mama, who would be weary from washing. She dreaded to go home. Things were quieting down. The little kids had stopped crying. Skeets went to the cistern for more water.

Oren picked up his book, which opened to an illustrated page on slick, coated paper. He showed it to Maureen. "How would you like to visit this place?"

She had never seen such a picture before. "What is it supposed to be?"

"It's a big church in France."

Just because she lived in Dotzero, Uncle Millard's kids

thought they could tell her anything, and she'd believe it. "I know good and well there's no such real building. You couldn't make a thing like that out of anything, not even cake icing."

Oren pointed to the caption: *Plate VI, Reims Cathedral, 13th Century, France.* "They did make it." He opened the book's front cover: "It says so in this book that belonged to H. W. Wiley."

"Henry Wadsworth Wiley," Maureen said, "and there was William Cullen Wiley and—"

"How do you know so much about them?" Skeets interrupted.

"It's on the tombstones in the Wiley cemetery," Maureen said. "There are lots of interesting things around here. At this place, you have your own cemetery."

"Oh, now, isn't that wonderful!" Dessie sneered.

"Our own cemetery." Skeets snickered.

"We'll never want for another thing," Vido said with a sigh.

They all began to laugh, even the little children, who didn't know what was supposed to be funny. They kept laughing. What a way to treat company!

Walter knew Maureen was offended, so he tried to be helpful. "You never can tell what will happen around here," he said. "Mit got work at Stackhouses'. He might see the unicorn. Mr. Stackhouse keeps this old mare because once she had a unicorn colt. Maureen told me so."

"A unicorn!" Skeets exclaimed, setting off more laughter. Even Oren stopped reading to join in. Maureen felt like crawling under the porch.

"You're right, Walter. It only *seems* quiet around here," Oren said. "A lot's going on. Vido, you remember that story we had about those old Greeks? Watch out. You might get carried away by that bull, Epitome of Lower Upson."

Maureen's temper flared. She didn't intend to stay with a batch of cousins who lied and laughed at company. However, she wasn't so angry that she forgot her manners. She started inside to tell Aunt Cora good-bye.

With a soapy rag, Skeets drew designs in the grime around the door facing. "I cleaned that hand-painted picture in your sitting room," Maureen said to her. "I'll bet you never saw one before."

"Did so. I saw a whole art museum full of 'em. Our art teacher took us there. I could make a painting myself if I had paints."

"You could not. You've got to be born talented to make hand-painted pictures." The broken screen flapped as Maureen banged the door behind her.

A mop lifted from dirty water had left marks like cat faces on the new linoleum. In the room off the kitchen, Aunt Cora seemed to be asleep on the lumpy bed, so Maureen tiptoed to the doorway of the sitting room to admire the wallpaper.

She was shocked. Low on one wall, black and brown crayon scribbles marred the garlands of roses. She hurried to the back door. "Skeets, the little kids have marked the new wallpaper."

"I know. Used up all my black and brown." Skeets acted as if ruining beautiful new wallpaper didn't matter.

41

She stopped slopping water on the door facing and looked at Maureen. "Maybe in a place like this, those marks will just disappear." Maureen was sure there was a smirk on Skeets's face.

"You'll never get that dirt off without elbow grease," Maureen whispered to Skeets. "You'll be messing around for a week if you don't use it."

"We don't have any. Can we borrow some from you?"

"No, you get it at Stackhouses' store," Maureen whispered behind her hand. "It's the only thing they have free. They keep it in a barrel out back, but don't let on to them I told you." Maureen stepped out on the porch, straightened her shoulders and ignored the giggling. "Walter and I have to go home and help with the work."

"Come again, Maureen," Dessie called after her, "and tell us more about the wonders of this place. Watch out for the gates."

Maureen didn't need to bother about gates. She was ready to roll under the new fence of the Wiley pasture when she saw Epitome of Lower Upson. He raised his great, horned white head and looked at her. He was blocky as a boxcar. His curly coat was as dark red as sweet cherries. Uncle Millard was nowhere in sight. Maureen walked on beside the fence as if she had noticed nothing.

Walter held up the fence strand. "Here's our place, Maureen. I'll hold it for you first."

"Can't you see Mrs. Wiley's bull over there?" She kept her voice low. "We're going up the lane a ways." She hoped their cousins watching from the porch wouldn't notice their change of route. She didn't want them to know that she was wary of anything on the place.

Epitome seemed calm enough, and generally Hereford cattle were gentle. But he was a very highbred bull, he was in a new place, and they were strangers to him. Besides, Tisket was along. Bulls didn't care much for small dogs.

"It's a long piece home by the lane and back road, and it's getting hotter," Walter complained.

"We don't have to go all the way home by the road. I know a little neck of the Wiley pasture that's close to our woods. We'll cross there and go to our ridge field."

"Are you afraid of Epitome of Lower Upson?"

"He's a pedigreed animal, Walter, and I don't want to make him nervous. You'd better not come to Uncle Millard's again by yourself. We don't know Epitome. I'll tell you something else, Walter. Uncle Millard's kids used to come here to visit for a day every summer, it's true, and we sent them apples and cards at Christmas. But we don't know them very well. No use blabbing everything you know to that covey of cousins."

"They are our own kin," Walter pointed out. "Skeets is going to teach me to stand on my head."

A curve in the lane brought them near timbered land. Epitome was out of sight far behind them. They hurried across the strip of pasture and followed the fence of McCrackens' woods to the ridge field that grew brown cockleburrs and dingy green cups of Queen Anne's lace.

Suddenly Maureen stopped. A red apple lay at her feet.

She picked it up and looked at a small tree in the fence corner. It's low limbs were heavy with beautiful fruit. "Walter, look here!"

He was puzzled. "This isn't the orchard. What's an apple tree doing here?"

"It's not supposed to be here." Maureen polished the apple on her dress until it shone like a ruby. It cracked with crispness when she bit into it. A sweet juice filled her mouth. As she chewed, the apple tasted even better. She handed it to Walter. "Sock your teeth into that."

A look of delight came over Walter's face as he ate the rest of the apple. "What kind is it, Maureen? Is it a Winesap or a Wealthy, or what?"

"It's a wild tree with no name." Maureen noted its location close to the Wiley pasture at the edge of Mc-Crackens' woods between a honey locust and a sassafras tree. "Take all we can now. Fill your pockets. We'll come back later for more. If Dad gets in a black mood, we'll have some on hand to surprise him and make him take heart. This tree just happened. It's one of those wonderful things you have to watch for. You never know when you'll run across one."

"We tried to tell our cousins that wonderful things can happen," Walter said.

"Most centainly, and they had no cause to laugh." Maureen grasped Walter's arm and caused him to drop two big apples. "Why didn't rabbits girdle this tree when it was little? Why didn't wood fires burn it up? Why didn't apple scale kill it? Dad and Mit hunt in these woods. They have plowed right there in our ridge field. It's been here long enough to have fruit. Why didn't somebody find it, somebody cutting wood? Why did we find it this very day?"

Walter smiled so broadly his eyes shut. "I'm sure glad we came around by the lane."

5

"There's something I want to settle with you, Maureen," Mama said the next morning, as she put the trivet holding the flatirons on the kerosene stove.

Maureen hoped a report of her visit to Uncle Millard's place might postpone, even eliminate, the settlement. "You wouldn't believe how they act over there," she began. "They don't play games or help with work, either. The big kids sit around and bellyache about not having hot sidewalks to walk on. All except Oren. He's always got his nose in a book. Aunt Cora doesn't make them mind, and she takes a nap in the morning. The little kids push each other around and squabble. That's not the worst, and I hate to tell you this. The little kids took—"

"Maureen," Mama broke in.

"They took Crayolas and marked up that pretty, clean

46

wallpaper," Maureen continued. "I don't think Aunt Cora bothered to give them a licking for it. Those big kids, including Skeets, who thinks she's big, told us a lot of dumb stuff and laughed at us."

Mama set up the ironing board. "About telling people things, Maureen. I understand that you told Skeets something yesterday."

"Like Skeets saying she'd been in a regular palace," Maureen rushed on. "And Oren showed me a picture and claimed there was such a real church made out of stone lace. Skeets says any old time she wants to she can paint a picture."

"Maureen, shut up!" Mama was mad as a wet hen. "You hear me out. I was dog tired yesterday from putting out a big wash, and then I had to finish your job. If I'd had the strength I'd have used a peach-tree switch on you when you came slipping home the back way. Then this morning I took milk to Millard's early, and I learned that Skeets and the twins took a long, hot walk to Stackhouses' yesterday afternoon to ask for elbow grease. They'll be joshing about that at the store for many a day. You made your own kinfolk a laughingstock. I'm rested today, and you have some licks coming. Which do you want, two with my eyes open or three with them closed?"

Maureen's heart sank. "I don't want any, but I guess I'll get 'em anyhow. Worse yet, I know I should feel sorry that dumb Skeets believed my joke, but I don't. Nothing is the way I thought it would be before they came. . . . So, as long as I don't feel sorry, I guess you'd better give me three licks with your eyes closed."

Mama thought for a while. "I could. That might clear the air, but it wouldn't snap the beans. There's a full bushel there on the porch for you to do this afternoon. The rest of us will go swimming." She pointed to the irons. "You can start ironing now. I'll locate some old bathing suits and overalls for Cora and the kids to wear. It will be a good chance for Mit to come before he starts work."

"Oh, Mama," Maureen wailed. "I'd rather have three with 'em shut, or even open, and get it over with."

"I know, Maureen, but you'll have plenty of time later on for play and visiting. It's best all around if you remember now at the start to be mannerly to your kinfolks."

Maureen ironed, put clothes away, and peeled potatoes for noon dinner. She hoped Mama would be impressed, change her mind, and let her go swimming; but she didn't. Maureen couldn't appeal to Dad, who was gone for the day working on the extra gang.

After dinner, Maureen sniffed back tears as she sat on the porch facing a bushel of beans. Mama and Mit finished their rummaging for bathing clothes and started for the creek. Walter came out on the porch, wearing his swimming suit. Maureen had hidden hers so Mama couldn't lend it to anybody.

"I wish you were coming." Walter's eyes were sad as a hound's. "I think I can almost swim. I wanted you to show me once more."

"Skeets can show you."

"She can't swim. Can't none of them swim. Skeets told me."

"Well, then you'll have to save all of them when they start to drown."

That was a lot to put on Walter, but he hadn't offered to stay and help her. "And another thing. You'll have to watch out for Old Whisker. It stays in the deep swimming hole. Once when Mit was swimming there, he felt its whisker touch his foot."

"Mit says Old Whisker is just a big catfish, nothing to be afraid of," Walter said.

"I know," Maureen agreed, "but Mit didn't see it. Folks see only splashes and flashes, and they can't get a hook into Old Whisker, so I think it's a sort of water monster. Of course, there are water moccasins, snapping turtles, and other things that are poison in that swimming hole too." She looked up at Walter. "Well, go on with the rest. There they come from the Wiley place."

Walter hung back a few moments, then went off whistling to meet the others. Before long Maureen heard joyful shrieks and shouts echoing from Lost Creek.

She didn't look at the pods she broke and tried not to think of beans. She imagined she had caught Old Whisker, and the editor of the Beaumont *Banner* had come to interview her. She gave her answers aloud. "I just made this big net out of a whole spool of bailer twine I had crocheted to make strong. I tied it to trees on the bank, and Old Whisker had just about pulled up the trees when I—"

"Whoo-hoo, anybody home?"

Maureen knew the voice and ran to meet her friend Rose Sansoucie.

49

"Oh, am I glad to see you!"

"First I thought everybody was down at the creek, from all the hollerin'. Then I heard somebody talking here."

"I was thinking of something and wanted to see how it sounded out loud." Maureen could tell her such things, and Rose wouldn't think she was crazy. "I'm the only one home."

The girls went to the shade of the porch, and Rose took off her straw hat. The stenciled flowers on its wide brim had chipped to traces of bright paint. She wore the hat all summer long, but she tanned brown as a biscuit anyhow. Her hair was glossy black and her eyes were brown as horse chestnuts.

The Sansoucies were the last family to live at the Wiley place before Uncle Millard came. When Rose's father got farm work at Cold Spring and they moved away, Maureen missed all of them.

"I split out and walked all the way," Rose said. "It took some managing to get over here without dragging some of the little kids along. I just begged and begged to come to see you before school starts. How come you're not down at the creek with the rest?"

"Somebody has to do the work," Maureen said primly. "Dad's got days on the extra gang. Mit's going to start work for Mr. Stackhouse, but I'm about the only one to work here at the house. I have to do the canning and everything. Mama is always chasing off to Uncle Millard's to wait on them. Or else down at the creek. She's hardly ever home."

"When you wrote and told me your uncle's family was coming, I thought you'd be over there playing all the time. All those games we used to play there—prison base, lemonade, rotten egg."

"They waste their time and complain." Maureen imitated a whining voice. "It's too hot. Nothing but trees."

"How about Crystal, the one our age?" Rose asked.

"You'd think she was more Walter's age from the size of her. She tries to take him over. Everybody thinks she's so special, such a card, just a half-pint. Like staying a runt is real wonderful. Even my dad thinks she's weak as a cat, and he gave her a piggyback ride once."

Rose was puzzled. "What is it that makes her special?"

"She's double-jointed for one thing." Maureen braced her arm on the step beside her. "Instead of her arm being straight like this, it bows out like it was broken. You have to stand aside, or she'll knock you over turning cartwheels. Skin-the-cat, she's good at that, too. Aunt Cora doesn't make her be ladylike. She draws all over everything and says she can hand paint pictures."

"Maybe she could teach you how," Rose pointed out.

"And maybe she wasn't born talented. Anyhow, we've got no paints. She's too hoity-toity to use Crayolas. The little kids use them on wallpaper. One thing she can't do do is swim, and I'm not going to teach her, either. If I showed her one stroke, first thing you know, she'd swim Lost Creek, Big River, the Meramec, and the entire Mississippi. That's the way she is. A regular show-off."

"You don't seem to be getting much good out of your

cousins, Maureen. I wish Skeets was around so I could see if she's as bad as you say."

"You won't miss anything if you don't see her." Maureen snapped beans. "Skeets is the worst-spoiled kid in the Saint Francois Mountains. Mama claims that in a big family it's hard to have a spoiled one. Don't believe it. They picked one to spoil, and she's it."

Maureen looked up at Rose and was surprised to see her mouth twisted as if she was trying not to smile. "Why are you looking like that?"

Rose let out her laugh. "I think you're jealous. You're the only girl in your family. Not like me. The Dotzero teachers always bragged on you. So did your grandma, and you had Walter all to yourself because Mit is a lot older than he is. Now you're kind of pushed out of the picture, and Skeets is painting the picture."

"That's no way for you to talk when you're company." Maureen was indignant. "You don't know anything about it. If it wasn't for Skeets being such a greenhorn, I'd be down there running with the rope, swinging out over the water, and jumping into Lost Creek instead of sitting here sweating and snapping these dumb beans."

Maureen felt miserable. Even Rose had sided with Skeets, sight unseen.

"Oh, now, we'll soon get these done." Rose took a handful of beans. "If you line them up on a dough board and cut them with a knife, they go faster."

Maureen went inside and got a board and two knives from the kitchen. The girls worked in silence for a while.

"I just told you that I believed you might be jealous because I'm your friend, and I didn't think you'd get mad," Rose said. "You're a better friend to me than anybody in Cold Spring. A friend to our whole family. I didn't aim to make you mad, Maureen."

"Oh, I know you didn't."

"If you've got jealous feelings gnawing at you that way, best get rid of them." Rose whacked down with the knife. "You feel bad if you're holding something against somebody."

Maureen tossed bean ends into the yard. "How do you get rid of jealous feelings? You can't toss them out like throwing scraps to the chickens."

"You'll figure it out, Maureen."

"I'd better." Maureen looked into the distance up toward McCrackens' woods. "Oh, Rose, Walter and I found something I want to show you. Unless you see it, you won't believe it."

"All right. Let's get these things done." Rose felt down into the basket. "Almost to the bottom."

It was good to have a chance to walk to the top of the ridge field with Rose. When they came to the edge of McCrackens' woods, they sat down in the shade of a black oak tree and rested. A squirrel barked in the treetop, and a flock of crows flapped and cawed at the edge of the field.

Maureen picked up an acorn. "Dad says these will fall into our field and sprout. Then it will go back to brush. We'll be living in a wilderness without stock to graze or mules to cultivate. When he talks like that, he gets into a blackness that's just awful. I want to keep our find a secret so I can surprise him with it if he gets gloomy. Now come along here. It's near the fence corner of our woods and the Wiley pasture."

Maureen had no trouble locating the apple tree between the honey locust and the sassafras. She picked a beautiful apple from a low branch for Rose.

A look of pleased surprise came over Rose's face as she tasted it. "I never had a better apple."

"I know. It's a wild tree. Probably the birds dropped the seed. It might be the best apple in the world," Maureen said very seriously.

"It was real nice of you to give me a taste, Maureen. Your dad will sure perk up when he knows this grows on your place." A train whistled. "There's Number 32. I promised I'd start home when it went through. I'll go over the ridge from here."

"You came at the right time, Rose. Here, take another apple."

Rose shook her head. "I don't think you can spare any more. You've got a lot of people who won't believe it unless they taste it. I'll get some next year when the tree is bigger."

Maureen went with Rose along the ridge above the field and pasture, then watched her go down the narrow wagon track until her straw hat looked no bigger than a mushroom. She had moved away a long time ago, but Maureen still missed her.

Maybe Uncle Millard's family missed friends they had left. That thought slackened the grip of the green-eyed monster that held Maureen. Even if that monster was bigger than Old Whisker, she'd get away from it and give it a kick in the pants, Maureen decided.

.6

Maureen actually looked forward to the start of school. Her cousins would rely on her for the proper way to behave in a one-room school, and Mrs. Nolen, the sole teacher, would depend on her for information about them.

On the first day of school, Maureen thought Mrs. Nolen looked as stylish as any town teacher. Her thick brown hair was brushed into a smooth roll like a baloney sausage around her head. Her skirt was long, which Maureen knew was in fashion from her study of the Sears catalog.

Right away, Mrs. Nolen made a big fuss over Uncle Millard's kids. She let Boots and Buddy dust erasers three days in a row. When Dessie leafed through eighth-grade books and said she'd already had everything in them, Mrs. Nolen let her take second graders to the cloakroom and help them with their reading.

Skeets drew in the margins of her books, but Mrs. Nolen never seemed to notice. Instead of working arithmetic story problems about Farmer Brown, she drew a picture of him and his fruit stand.

Maureen estimated that Skeets drew about 60 percent of the time and had scribbled in 100 percent of her books. The sixth grade was studying percent, which Maureen considered a great improvement over fractions. She liked to think of things in nice round hundreds. Percent was as tidy as long division that came out even.

She was sure that the arithmetic she had just finished would be marked 100 percent. Now she could listen to the eighth-grade civics class.

"We are fortunate to have Oren, who has lived in a city, in our class for this unit," Mrs. Nolen said. "Now what do we call the head of city government?"

Oren waved his hand as usual. "The mayor," he answered.

Maureen was embarrassed for Oren. Everybody knew that a mare was a lady horse. They'd laugh at him more than they had at Skeets when she asked for elbow grease.

"Correct, Oren," Mrs. Nolen said in a syrupy sweet voice she used for all Uncle Millard's kids.

At afternoon recess, Skeets was chosen first for wolf-over-the-ridge, a game she didn't know how to play. But she caught on and ran fast with her yellow hair flying. Maureen hoped she wouldn't make a diaper out of her dress and show off turning cartwheels. It was a relief when Mrs. Nolen rang the bell ending recess.

Except for percent, the first week of school had disappointed Maureen. She hadn't even had a chance for a good talk with Mrs. Nolen, so she decided to stay after school.

"Walter and I will help you straighten up and sweep out, Mrs. Nolen," Maureen offered. "Where's that oily sawdust to sprinkle around to keep down dust?"

Mrs. Nolen picked up her lunch box and a pile of papers. "Thanks, that's nice of you, because I'm tired clear through, even my voice. But we can go home. I'm not janitor this year. Stackhouses have their nephew, Melvin, from Beaumont staying with them. So Sterling Stackhouse hired him for the job." There were clumping and banging noises like a dozen people in the cloakroom. "He's here, right on the job."

Maureen went to the cloakroom door. "Well, good-bye, Mrs. Nolen. Just think, only about 97 percent more school this year. I figured it out."

Walter squeezed by the youth working in the cloakroom. Maureen watched him sweep; he wasn't a bit handy with a broom. Most likely he'd never dust anything.

She went outside and saw Walter running to catch up with Skeets. "Walter, come back here," she called. "We have to go ask for mail."

Slowly Walter returned, and they went down the school hill together. In the store window, Walter noticed a poster picturing a Ferris wheel. "What's that?"

"Read it yourself; you're in third grade."

"And you're awful cranky, Maureen."

"I am not," she snapped. "I might go blind someday,

58

and then I couldn't do all your reading. You have to learn to take care of yourself."

Walter leaned over the porch railing to look down the road where Uncle Millard's kids were still in sight.

"Oh, well, don't go away mad." Maureen put her arms around Walter's shoulders and turned him toward the poster. "This tells about the Beaumont County Fair, September 14 to 18, 1937," Maureen read: "Agricultural and home economics exhibits—livestock, poultry, horticulture, pomology. Valuable premiums in all classes. Midway entertainment for the whole family. All-day admission twenty-five cents, children under twelve, fifteen cents."

"Are we going?" Walter asked.

"Not this fall. Last year Mama got first prize for Molly's butter, but we wouldn't have a pound to spare now. Nothing's the same."

"What's pomology?" Walter asked.

"You expect me to know everything. The eighth grade hasn't had that yet." Maureen let the screen bang as they went into the store.

Others from school had stopped there, and both Mr. and Mrs. Stackhouse were busy. Finally Mrs. Stackhouse puffed up to Maureen. "I guess you're next."

"Any mail for McCracken?" Maureen asked the routine question.

"Mail? No, but we've got in some large kraut crocks. You folks might need extra." Mrs. Stackhouse sat down on a stool behind the counter. "Did you learn anything at school today, Maureen?"

"Learned a mare is something beside a colt's mama," Maureen reported. "It's the head of a city."

Mrs. Stackhouse nodded. "Pronounced the same, but spelled differently." She seemed quite well informed.

"What does pomology mean?" Maureen asked.

"Oh, it means fruits—apples, pears, quince. Now you've learned something else." Mrs. Stackhouse straightened a stack of school tablets on the counter. "I guess you already knew that Mit is a two-fisted eater. We've found that out. Sterling says we've got to give that boy his dinner as part of his job. We're giving him a trip to the fair next week, too. Sterling is showing our best Duroc hogs and needs help with hauling. We do what we can. There was Sterling's brother, Jo Shelby Stackhouse, in Beaumont with all those children, nothing for the big strapping ones to do, and us without chick or child. So we're having Melvin and Hazel stay with us. I think we should give young people a chance even if it does mean extra cooking, washing, and tracking in mud."

"We saw Melvin janitoring at school," Maureen said.

"Hazel ought to be around someplace." Mrs. Stackhouse looked toward the store's wareroom. "She's supposed to help here and at the house. Hazel spends more time in front of the looking glass than in front of the dishpan. She keeps the hair-curling iron stuck in the lamp chimney. When she uses the flatiron, she only takes pains with her own clothes, folds up the sheets unironed if I don't watch her."

"I've been doing a lot of work at home," Maureen said.

60

"I helped with canning. Let's see, we have. . . ." Walter, ready to leave, tugged impatiently at Maureen's hand, but she wanted to try using percent. "I'd say we have 82 percent of our canning done. Just about everything but apple butter. We're doing that tomorrow."

"Any mail for O'Neil?" Walter had never piped up like that at the store before.

"Yes, I was expecting that little Skeets to breeze in here for it. It's a postal card for Cora. Lorene, who worked with her at the hat factory, wants to say hello." Mrs. Stackhouse threw back her head and called, "Haaaazel."

The girl who appeared at the wareroom door was a few years older than Maureen but not much taller. Her brown hair was a spring of corkscrew curls. A red-orange circle glowed on each cheek.

"Hazel, save me some steps and get that card out of the O'Neil pigeonhole for Maureen." As Hazel passed her, Mrs. Stackhouse fanned with her hand as if suffocated by the fragrance of her face powder and perfume.

"I like your rouge," Maureen fibbed, as she took the card from Hazel at the post-office window.

"Tangee. I sent off for a free sample." Hazel chewed her gum and popped it.

"My brother Mit works for your uncle. I guess you know him."

"Yeah, but I don't think he knows I'm livin'. Never says anything to me. He's awful quiet."

"Not at home. He's always yelling about something," Maureen said. She thought of Mit's recent unreasonable

61

demand that his overalls be ironed. Also he changed his shirt twice as often as Dad did. She had an idea that Mit wanted to look good to Hazel, even if he didn't talk to her.

Hazel took an opened package of gum from her skirt pocket. "Have a stick of Juicy Fruit." She nodded toward Walter. "Take one for him."

Walter was talking up again. Maureen heard him ask Mrs. Stackhouse what had become of all Patsy's colts. She hustled him right out of the store.

Walter reached for the card. "Gimme the mail. I'll run and maybe catch up with Skeets."

Maureen held the card high. "No need to break your neck running after her. We don't have to wait on them hand and foot. If this wasn't United States mail, I'd throw it in the creek when we cross. But I guess I'll give it to them tomorrow. I hope my job then is picking apples, but I'm not showing anybody that wild tree we found."

Abruptly Maureen had an idea, and she grabbed Walter by the shoulders. "Do you know what we're going to do? We're going to put that wonderful apple in the pomology exhibit at the Beaumont Fair. It'll get first prize, a blue ribbon and prize money besides. I'll bring in a little something."

"How will we get to Beaumont with the apples, Maureen?"

She studied the problem for a few moments. "We're going in the Stackhouse truck. I think we can fit in the cab with Mr. Stackhouse and Mit, even if you are a little chubby."

Maureen planned as they walked on down the road. "I'll have to do some tall talking for Dad and Mama to let us miss a day of school. I can't tell them about the apple ahead of time. That's all going to be a surprise. They'll be just flabbergasted. All Uncle Millard's family will be too. We can make up our schoolwork, and I'll give a special report on the pomology exhibit. Walter, I'd say we have an 85 percent chance to get to the fair."

7 _____

Maureen awoke in her room at the top of the stairs and listened to morning sounds from the kitchen below. The oven door hinge squeaked as Mama put biscuits in to bake. The back screen slammed. A bucket rattled. Dad was straining Molly's milk. The clunk of footsteps on the cellar steps and the clink of glass brought her right out of bed. Mit was bringing up the last of the empty half-gallon jars for apple butter canning.

She'd get right downstairs and be dependable. If she was to be allowed to go to the fair and win first prize for her discovered apple, she'd have to be a wonder of work all day long.

She dressed quickly. Her faded dress was outgrown, and her cotton stockings had holes. But they'd do for Saturday. Maureen went to the room the boys shared and shook Walter awake. Then she took the steps two at a time down to the kitchen.

"I'll fry the eggs, Mama," she offered, "so you can take up biscuits and pour milk and coffee."

Maureen was careful not to break the yolk of the egg she served Mit. He was in a hurry to have breakfast and be off to work. Maureen thought he might be anxious to see Hazel Stackhouse and wondered what she could find out by teasing. She took her place at the table. "I hope Hazel Stackhouse gives you a fine dinner, Mit. Is she a good cook?"

Mit gulped down a glass of skim milk. "Opens a lot of cans from the store."

"Do you think she's pretty?"

Mit shook his head.

"Then she must be smart," Maureen speculated.

"Not very." Mit buttered another biscuit. "What's it to you?"

"I'm trying to figure out why you're struck on her."

Mit jumped up from the table ready to collar Maureen.

"Sit down, Mit," Dad ordered. "I want to talk business with you. When's payday?"

"Mr. Stackhouse didn't say."

Dad looked worried. "How much is he paying you?"

"He said he'd make it right with me." Mit finished another biscuit.

Dad's troubled look deepened. "That's a mite uncertain."

"I figure I'm lucky to get paid work and my dinner besides." Mit got up from the table and had a final look at himself in the kitchen mirror.

Mama started to clear the table. "Much obliged for bringing the fruit jars up, Mit. We'll miss you this year, but you've got other work now, and we've got more hands. Cora wants to boil the apples down at the Wiley place where it's easier for Vido to look after the little ones."

As Mama washed dishes, she looked out the kitchen window at Dad and Mit setting off down the hill. "I declare, Mit's so anxious to work, the days aren't long enough."

"He's anxious to see Hazel Stackhouse," Maureen said, as she dried dishes. "She gets herself so fixed up that he couldn't miss her. He won't admit it, but I think he's struck on her too, Mama. Why else would he tell me I had to iron his overalls? He's always changing his shirt so he won't smell sweaty. Why doesn't he talk to her, be nice to her?"

Mama washed the biscuit mixing bowl. "If you're right, Maureen, he might be so afraid of saying the wrong thing that he's tongue-tied. Up until now, he's teased girls, bossed them around. Now maybe he feels different, and he's not sure why."

"He doesn't know how to start to be nice. Had no practice," Maureen said.

Mama smiled. "And he doesn't want to make a fool of himself."

"I guess he wants to do something besides spit a long way to impress Hazel, but he might as well own up to liking her." Maureen spread the dish towel on the drying rack. "Now that we've got dishes done I'm ready for an outside job. I'll pick up windfalls. I need Walter."

"All right. I've toted apples to Millard's all week, but we can use more. I'll send somebody back to add to your windfall crew."

Mama rattled marbles in her apron pocket. She'd borrowed them from Walter to roll with the stirring stick in the bottom of the kettle to keep the apple butter from sticking and scorching. She shouldered the L-shaped stirring stick. It was long-handled so that the tender of the outdoor kettle could stand back from the fire and the plop of boiling sauce.

"I guess I've got everything including Cora's card. Now scoot down cellar and get your baskets." Mama set off for Uncle Millard's.

When Maureen and Walter opened the door to the cellar where they had hidden their special apples, a wonderful fragrance came up from the cool dimness. "Our apple smells extra good. Breathe deep, Walter." Maureen inhaled the apple-scented air.

She pointed to a list penciled on the cellar side of the door. It was a record of the bushels they had stored from their orchard the previous year. Maureen liked the names of the varieties. She pointed and read, "Winesap, Wolf River, Ben Davis, Winter Banana, Maiden's Blush, Sheepnose, Disharoon."

"Are we going to write down our apple?" Walter asked.

"Someday. We'll have to think of a name for it."

They brought up three bushel baskets that would have

been easy to carry nested together if Walter hadn't been so short.

Maureen and Walter crossed the barn lot to the orchard. The sun had already dried the dew on the tall grass that was plumed with seed and buzzing with cicadas. Fallen apples made the orchard smell like cider.

It was so nice in the orchard that filling the first basket hardly seemed like work. Maureen heard rustling and had to look twice to see Skeets. Her head was the same color and not much higher than the seeded grass. Right there in their own orchard as boss of the windfall crew Maureen might have the opportunity she needed to feel better about Skeets.

"I'm all stuck up." Skeets sat down under the York Imperial apple tree and began to pick burrs off her overalls.

Maureen held up a badly bruised apple. "This isn't good enough for apple butter. It might do for cider. We've got two more baskets to fill."

"Okay. First I'll get these burrs off." Skeets tugged at big burdock stickers.

Maureen wondered why Skeets didn't get burrs in her hair with it flying around so. "Hurry up, Skeets, latch on to the side of this basket and help me carry it to the gate."

As they struggled up the orchard slope, the wire handle cut into Maureen's hand. She was relieved when Skeets asked to rest and change hands.

On the way down again, Skeets ran off like a scared rabbit and disappeared.

"Hi, Maureen," a voice came from overhead. There was Skeets at the very top of a big Smokehouse apple tree.

"We're not supposed to pick from the trees. What are you doing up there?"

"Looking around. Things look different up here. It's nice; come on up."

Maureen didn't intend to let Skeets know that she got very dizzy and scared in high places. "We've got work to do," she grumbled.

Skeets finally came down and started to help. Suddenly she shrieked, shook her right hand, and hopped around on one foot. Maureen grabbed her hand. A white welt with a red dot in the center swelled on the back.

"A yellow jacket stung you." Thoughts of a yellow-jacket sting made Maureen's scalp crawl, but she tried to make little of the pain. "They are always around fallen fruit, trying to get sweet juice."

"O-o-o-h," Skeets wailed.

"You have to watch out for them." Maureen pointed to a low spot between rows of trees. "There's a little spring over there. Get some mud and put it on that sting. Mud will take the fire right out of it."

"No! Mud's not medicine. I'm going home." Skeets held out her hand, which was swelling like a biscuit in a hot oven.

"If you won't do anything to help yourself, Skeets, you might as well," Maureen agreed.

"I want Walter to go with me," Skeets sobbed.

"He can't. He has to stay and help me." Maureen gave Walter a look that she hoped was stern.

"Come on, Walter. Vido will know what to do." Skeets started up the orchard hill. Walter tagged after her.

Maureen worked alone and watched for yellow jackets. She had been stung by everything that packed a stinger—wasps, bees, hornets. She cringed to think of them. Still, she thought Skeets had made an awful fuss over that sting.

She hadn't done well with her crew: one worker hurt, another disobedient. She might not get to go to the fair if things didn't improve. She wondered if the apples on the wild tree were any redder. One thing sure, no one would miss her if she went to see.

She followed the fence line of McCrackens' woods, for she knew it would lead to her apple tree. Taking her time, she watched a flock of cedar waxwings divide and take turns swallowing the red berries of a dogwood tree. A flock of blackbirds rose from a thicket of sumac, swooped down again, spread apart, came together, flew to a little persimmon, and set the whole tree atwitter.

In the distance Epitome bellowed. With new posts and barbed wire, she had no fear of him, even though her tree was just beyond the fence. The honey locust was in sight.

The bellowing was angry and very close. Maureen saw a huge red hulk struggling on the ground. One fence post was pulled out, one snapped off, and the barbed-wire strands were loose. A few seconds passed before Maureen realized what had happened. The wire was tangled around Epitome's jerking legs. One strand was across his back. He looked as helpless as a derailed boxcar.

With each kick, he drove the sharp barbs into his hide and tangled the wire around his neck. He threw his great horned head from side to side and rolled his eyes so that the whites showed. If Epitome kept struggling, he would kill himself.

She pulled on the wire. Epitome flung his massive head in terror. A horn barely missed Maureen's chest.

There wasn't time to run to the Wiley place to try to locate Uncle Millard for help. Maureen remembered he had returned the wire stretchers and the wire cutters. She herself had braved the smells of a corner of the packing shed to put them away.

She knew what she had to do. In no time, she was over the rough, rocky ground of the ridge field. At the packing-shed door, she pulled hard on the rope of the bell. Ordinarily she held her nose when she went into the part of the shed that smelled like rancid fish and rotten eggs. Whale-oil soap and yellow sulphur powder for spraying fruit trees were stored there. Now she plunged right in, tumbling over a grass seeder and a spray tank, to find the wire cutters. She yanked the bell rope again and started back uphill with the heavy cutters.

_8

Maureen's breath caught in her throat as she ran to Epitome and found him in a worse tangle than ever. Blood oozed from the barbed-wire cuts on his back. A patch of flies clustered on his broad withers. Maureen moved slowly toward him with outstretched cutters. Cattle smell was close. Flies swarmed up in her face.

"Easy now, easy, old boy." Maureen spoke low and soothingly, as Dad did around stock. "Easy, Epitome of Lower Upson."

She pushed hard on the handles to snap the cutter and sever the wire. Epitome tried to get up on his hind legs, but he was still held down. Since he'd been pastured near Uncle Millard's he ought to be used to kids, but Maureen didn't know how he would behave when hurt and scared.

72

Once free, he might turn on her as the cause of his pain. But she had to get him loose.

"I'll get you out. Easy, easy, Epitome," she chanted.

Epitome got his hindquarters up but fell headlong again with his front legs still entangled. His great sides heaved. Two more cuts of wire, and he would be able to stand. Maureen was set to run and climb the sassafras tree. The cutters snapped once, twice. With a heaving effort, Epitome got up on all fours. He pawed the ground and stamped the wire. Maureen circled around him, reached over, and pulled the wire entanglement away from his short legs. Epitome was free.

He wheeled toward her and lowered his horned head. The wire tangle and the standing part of the fence now blocked her way to the sassafras tree. There wasn't time to run. She stood still, still as a post. She didn't even breathe. Epitome gave a final bellow, turned, and walked stiffly away into the pasture.

Maureen collapsed on the ground. Her heart pumped wildly. Voices shouted her name, so the farm bell had been heard. She gave a weak yoo-hoo in reply.

Skeets, who could run fastest, reached her first and was mystified to see her lying on the ground. "What happened? Are you stung, or what?"

"I nearly got killed by a bull," Maureen whispered. Skeets bent over her and looked for wounds.

Mama came running and knelt beside her. "Are you bad hurt, Maureen? You're white as a sheet. Anything broken?" Gently she moved Maureen's arms.

"Not hurt. About scared to death." Maureen began to sob.

Mama gathered Maureen into her arms. "The fence is all ripped out. What was it, hon?"

With Mama's help, she got shakily to her feet and hung onto the nearest standing fence post. "Epitome got himself all tangled up in fence wire. I used the wire cutters and cut him out before he killed himself. He was bellowing and swinging that big head of his around. I thought sure he'd come at me soon as he got loose."

"You did the right thing, and that took some nerve." Mama looked at the trampled ground and tangled wire. "He sure tore up jack around here. He was set to ruin himself, pedigree or no pedigree. Mrs. Wiley is going to be surprised to know who rescued her valuable bull."

To attract her attention, Walter tugged at Maureen's hand. "I'll tell you about it after a while, Walter," she said. "Keep hold of Tisket. Epitome might still be riled up."

"Doesn't appear to be. He's down in the far pasture now, behaving himself as usual." Mama shook a wobbly post. "It looks like he tried to jump the fence. I wonder what got into him."

Walter was pulling at Maureen again. He showed her a crushed apple and pointed urgently through the break in the fence.

"He's ruined it!" Maureen screamed. "Epitome broke off our wonderful apple tree."

The top of the little tree hung to the ground from a jagged break in the trunk. Apples were trampled and crushed into the earth around the broken tree.

74

"He's just ruined the apple tree that Walter and I found. I wish I had let him kill himself. He's got a pedigree, but he's got no manners at all," Maureen wailed. "He ate all the apples on the limb near the fence. Then he jumped the fence and pulled down the tree to get the rest. He's more of a hog than a bull."

Mama tasted a crushed apple. "I can't blame him. This has fine flavor. I think he got in trouble when he tried to jump back over the fence to be with the herd. I guess he was heavier and didn't clear the top strand of wire. His pedigreed legs were too short."

Aunt Cora nibbled on a bit of apple, which was easier for her with her missing tooth than biting into whole fruit. "Anybody would be pleased to find this. Now, Maureen, don't fret that you lost it. Remember what Paul wrote to the Philippians: 'I know both how to be abased, and I know how to abound.'"

Mama had never known a wild tree on the place to get to bearing size. Usually range stock grazed off the sprouts or blight killed them.

Uncle Millard examined the splintered tree. "I didn't see this when I worked just a few feet away. I was looking, too, the way I've been doing since I started my reading. We've got a regular library of Wiley books. I was reading Henry David Thoreau, but I'll have to stop now to fix the fence. I wish I could fix your tree, Maureen, but it's beyond fixing."

"Nobody saw it except Walter and me." Maureen put her arm around Walter's shoulders. "We were going to keep it for a surprise."

Dessie threw away a core. "Apples. Well, we've got a world of apples. About all we have got. There's plenty left."

"But we found it, and it was special," Maureen said.

"You saved Epitome, and that was special," Mama said. Suddenly she thought of something. "Oh, heavens, we forgot the apple butter kettle."

Maureen didn't try to keep up with the others. Her knees felt wobbly; she'd had enough running for one day.

The fire had died down under the kettle so that the apple butter had not burned. Mama stirred the thickening sauce and assigned jobs. Since Maureen wasn't given any, she joined Skeets, who was on the porch dabbing her hand with a damp cloth.

"Does it still hurt?" Maureen asked.

"It itches now, but it's getting better. Vido put this camphor on it." She held out her hand. "It's so swelled I can't hold a pencil."

"A little yellow jacket hurt you worse than that half-ton bull hurt me."

Skeets held the cloth on her hand. "It must have been awful scary."

"It was no pussycat in the yarn basket," Maureen assured her.

That evening when Dad and Mit came home, Maureen told of rescuing Epitome. To make the story interesting, she played the parts of both herself and the bull.

"You don't need to get down on the floor like that. Be ladylike," Mama said.

Dad listened carefully. "You must have talked to him right."

"Just easy, easy, the way you do, Dad."

When Maureen told him about the apple, Dad smacked his lips. "I can almost taste it. All the wild apples I've ever known were knobby, sour, pithy things, not even fit for cider. I didn't know we had a bearing wild tree on the place, and I've hunted squirrel, quail, and rabbit up there. Thought I knew every inch of that land. I wish it had been back in the woods, away from the fence."

They wondered how deep the cuts were in Epitome's back and planned to take some of the scarce shelled corn away from the hens and lure him into the barn to doctor him with ointment. Otherwise, flies would lay eggs in the cuts.

"Now wouldn't you wonder why the Almighty created flies to torment a hurt beast?" Dad shook his head, and Maureen wished she had some magic to head off the dark look that came over his face.

"I don't question the ways of the Almighty," Mama said. "Anyhow, barbed wire was what cut the bull's back. The Almighty didn't create barbed wire."

"We'll do what we can for him," Dad said. "Mrs. Wiley claims he's the best Hereford bull in the county, and she's planning to show him at the fair."

Maureen thought of the apples from the wild tree that she and Walter had hidden in the cellar. "We want to go to the fair too, Walter and I do. Mit's going. We could go in Stackhouses' truck. Please!"

Mama and Dad looked at each other in a way that meant agreement. "That's reasonable enough, considering how handy you've been around here, rescuing a valuable bull," Dad said. "You showed a lot of gumption."

Mama nodded. "I think Maureen could do with a change of scenery. Here of late she's had more cares than a crawdad. You could visit with Grandma, Maureen. She'll be working at the Baptist lunch booth."

When Mama, Dad, and Mit went out to take care of Epitome, Maureen held to the back of a kitchen chair and jumped up and down. "We get to go, Walter. We'll win first prize for sure, and it will be a surprise after all. We've got enough apples to exhibit in that basket in the cellar. You see, you don't need a whole lot of anything, just a smidgen." Between her thumb and forefinger, she measured an inch of space. "It tells about that in Hurlbut's *Story of the Bible*. I can show you. No bigger than a mustard seed, it says. I believe in smidgens."

"Me too." Walter's broad smile almost closed his eyes.

9

On Monday, Maureen made sure that Mrs. Nolen understood why she and Walter would be absent the next day. She didn't want her to think they were home sick with something catching.

That evening she tried not to pester Mit when he came home tired and hungry. Finally he reported that she and Walter could go but cautioned Maureen that she must not utter one word on the way to Beaumont. Mr. Stackhouse didn't want any distracting talk when he was hauling good hogs.

Next morning Maureen was the first one up. No one saw her as, still in her nightgown and barefooted, she slipped down the shortcut path with a peck basket of apples, which she hid behind a tuft of tall grass.

Back in her room she dressed in her freshly ironed blue-checked gingham that wasn't much too short. All the shine was gone from her cracked patent-leather slippers. She glanced in the mirror and saw that her hair was already straightening. There was only a slight bump instead of the deep waves she had tried to create overnight with a head full of bobby pins.

Walter came in yawning, and Maureen inspected his clean overalls and starched white shirt. Mama surely had given him a short haircut. "Walter, you look fine," she said.

After breakfast, Mama counted out their coins, enough for admission, lunch at Grandma's booth, and ten cents extra. Maureen tied the money in the corner of her handkerchief and was glad her dress had a good pocket to put it in.

"Maureen, you and Walter come on, if you're coming," Mit called from the yard. "Mr. Stackhouse won't wait all day; he'll go without us."

They hurried down the shortcut path and caught up with Mit. "Want to see a magician's trick, Mit?" From the tall grass Maureen drew out a basket of glowing red apples.

Mit stopped to comb his hair. "Where did those come from?"

"Epitome didn't make applesauce out of these. We picked them the day we found our tree," Maureen explained. "We're putting them in the pomology exhibit. These apples have a 100-percent chance to get first-prize money."

"Gimme one." Mit reached into the basket.

"You just had breakfast." Maureen pulled the basket away.

"I know, but Mr. Stackhouse might not buy me much dinner at the fair."

"Just one, Mit. I don't know how many we need."

Mit chomped into the apple. "Man alive, this is good," he said between bites. "I guess you can spare another one." He took two more and hurried off down the path.

Maureen held Walter back. "Let him get out of reach. If this keeps up, we won't have enough."

At a slower pace, Maureen could enjoy the cool of the morning. Lost Creek willows were clouds of soft, dusty green. Along the road, sumac thickets were turning scarlet and buckbrush stems arched down with red berries. Robins flocked together in a chinquapin tree, but all the birds were still now that nesting time was over. Maureen felt happy to be up so early on her way to the fair. She recalled a Bible verse she'd heard Aunt Cora quote, "Joy cometh in the morning."

It wasn't quiet at the Stackhouse loading chute. Mr. Stackhouse whooped his hog call. The pigs grunted and squealed as Mit and Melvin prodded them up the ramp into the truck. Mrs. Stackhouse shouted advice. Hazel giggled with excitement.

Maureen didn't want Walter to get dirty around a drove of Duroc hogs, so she ordered him into the truck cab. As she got in, she carefully smoothed her dress to keep from wrinkling it when she sat down. There was just room enough across her lap and Walter's for the basket of apples.

Hazel came to the cab and offered Maureen and Walter gum. She was so carefully made up that she must have been working on her face for hours. Going to all that trouble showed she was boy crazy, Maureen decided, and Mit was the only boy Hazel's age around to be crazy about.

Maureen gave Mit half of her stick of gum when he got in the truck. "Hazel's always giving us gum. Trying to get on the good side of you by being nice to us. Mit, do you like Hazel?"

"I've got nothing against her," Mit said.

It wasn't a straight answer, but at least Mit hadn't collared Maureen for asking. When Mr. Stackhouse got in and started the motor, Maureen gave Hazel an extra-wide wave trying to make up for Mit, who sat stiff-necked as a sinner, looking straight ahead as if he, not Mr. Stackhouse, was the driver. As they pulled away, Maureen noticed that Mit looked up into the rearview mirror for a last glimpse of her.

There were more cars than usual on the narrow road to Beaumont. Luckily, most drivers recognized the Stackhouse truck and pulled to the side and stopped. Maureen chewed her gum nervously. Mr. Stackhouse drove in the middle of the road.

Near Beaumont fairground, the road was wider and dustier. Mr. Stackhouse drove to the livestock pavilion. To Maureen, the word *pavilion* seemed very fancy for a wide tin roof supported by poles. She and Walter left the confusion and mire of many trucks unloading livestock. They hurried by horses being exercised at the racetrack and glimpsed the sideshow tent going up on their way to the Hall of Horticulture.

This circular building with its bare wooden floor and sun-warmed wooden walls was Maureen's favorite at the fair. But it was too quiet there. They stepped inside to see exhibits of apples, pears, peaches, grapes all in place on the wide display shelf around the wall. Among the orderly mounds of tomatoes and peppers, a woman checked entry tags. Pinned to her dress was a badge with a green ribbon marked *Fair Committee*.

"Could you please tell me where to put these apples?" Maureen asked.

The woman looked at Maureen over the top of her glasses. "It's too late to enter now. Horticulture judging is starting soon."

"Too late!" Maureen was dismayed. "No, it can't be too late. The fair's not open yet. They're taking in pigs. We just brought some."

"Everything but livestock had to be entered yesterday, ready for folks to see when the fair opened today." She tapped her badge. "I ought to know. Didn't you have a book of regulations?"

"No, ma'am." Maureen was so disappointed that she almost whispered.

"That does look like nice fruit. Maybe I could get it in here." The woman moved paper plates of apples. "I could mark the tag *For Exhibit Only*, since you've come too late to compete. Now what variety is it?"

Maureen brightened. "It's a wild apple, so it's a new variety, hasn't got a name yet."

"That can't be a wild apple. It looks too good. If you don't know the variety, I can't put them in. It's printed right in the book of regulations. 'All varieties must be accurately labeled.' I can't make any exceptions to that." The woman rearranged the plates of apples. "Now I'll have to hurry and check all entry tags before the judge gets here."

On the doorstep of the hall, Maureen sank down without smoothing her dress to keep it from wrinkling. "Walter, I can hardly believe we've come this close and still can't get our apples in the fair to win first prize."

Walter sat beside her. "We're here anyhow. There are a lot of things to see. People are coming, so I guess it's started."

A group of people came purposefully toward the Hall of Horticulture. All wore green-ribbon badges except the man in the seersucker suit and Panama hat. He wore a purple ribbon marked *Judge*. Maureen and Walter moved aside to let them pass.

"You're right, Walter. We've got a lot to look at. I wish we didn't have to carry these apples around all morning."

"Maybe we could sell them," Walter suggested.

Maureen considered. "People spend their money on pop and cotton candy at the fair. They don't know how good these are. It would take all day to sell them and wouldn't be much fun. We might as well give them away. Here, put two in your pocket for us. The rest can be a surprise for people." Maureen held out an apple to a young woman wheeling a baby in a stroller. "Free sample, extra good apple."

The woman looked suspiciously at the apple and pushed on, but the next two people who came along took one. An old man sliced his with a pocketknife. "You're right, miss. This is the best apple I've ever tasted, and I've tasted a lot of 'em. You should have put it in the fair and won the prize."

"I know," Maureen agreed.

When the judge came out of the Hall of Horticulture with the Fair Committee, Maureen thought he glanced curiously at the three apples left in their basket. Maybe he would give a special award. She thrust a shining apple into his hand. The time had come to speak up.

"This apple tastes even better than it looks, and if you don't believe me, just try it. We brought some to put in the fair, but we couldn't on account of all the rules and regulations. Whatever you hung a blue ribbon on in there isn't as good as this."

The judge took off his Panama hat, and his sweaty hair stuck to his white forehead. "Have to learn about those regulations early. Go by the rules," he said.

"That's what I told her." The same woman was looking at her again over the top of her glasses. "We have to have a system, or we'd never get anything done."

"You'd get more done right without a system." Maureen hadn't intended to be so nervy, but she kept on. "Because this way, you didn't give the prize to the best apples that came to the fair."

"She seems mighty sure of herself." The judge winked at the group. "What variety is this?"

"It's a new discovered apple," Maureen declared. "Walter, my brother here, and I found it at the edge of our woods. I thought I would have a lot more than this, but—"

The judge took a bite of the apple. "H-m-m, wonderful flavor. Are you sure you didn't hear your mother or father say what variety this is?"

"No, because they didn't say." For a judge, he didn't seem to listen very carefully. "Like I told you, we discovered it new. We don't have many because this purebred bull—"

"Must be one of the older varieties still growing in an abandoned orchard," the judge decided.

"Nope, wasn't," Maureen kept on. "My dad planted our orchard, and he takes care of it there at our place at Dotzero on Lost Creek."

"I've heard about the fishing in Lost Creek. Big catfish." The judge looked at his watch. "I wish I had time to check this out, but I've got another fair to judge today, two counties over. Then I've got to get back to my job. Have you got a couple left? I'll take them along for my boss. He might know this variety."

"Sure. Take the rest, but he won't know it, either," Maureen assured him.

Mit appeared as the judge walked away. "Maureen, what do you think you're doing, sassing that judge?"

"I wasn't sassing him. Just trying to talk some sense into him, but it didn't do any good."

"Somebody told me kids were here peddling extra-good apples. You'll get in trouble. You have to have a permit to sell anything at a fair. Besides, I'd think you'd have more pride than to stand around selling apples, one by one, as if Dad and I didn't have work."

"I wasn't selling them. I was giving them away, Mit. No use to have something wonderful unless somebody knows about it. That's what a fair is for. That's why Mr. Stackhouse took a day off from the store and the farm to bring his pigs here."

Mit looked at the empty basket. "I see you can't give any more away. Now make sure you're at the truck at four o'clock, or we're going home without you. I've got to get back to the stock."

"I don't think he's having a very good time. He has to keep those pigs clean as pussycats until the swine judge shows up." Maureen grasped Walter's hand. "Come on, let's go to the church booth and see Grandma and leave this basket."

Grandma was busy making coffee and cutting pies, but she stopped and fussed over Maureen and Walter. When she hugged her, Maureen smelled Grandma's Evening in Paris perfume. She wore a flowered dress with a lace collar, and her ruffled organdy apron was prettier than the plain aprons of the other ladies.

They told her of their disappointment about entering the apple. Walter took one of the apples from his pocket for Grandma to try.

She took a taste. "It's on the order of a Roxbury Russet

but firm and tart as a Northern Spy. My, what an apple! It's a downright shame you lost it."

Grandma had coffee customers, so Maureen and Walter set off to see the fair. In the poultry exhibit they inspected chickens with feather topknots, hissing geese with knobs on their bills, white turkeys and bronze turkeys. Maureen had trouble getting Walter away from the pens of little Bantam chickens. She wanted to see the sheep and pat their soft, sheared backs.

They were going toward the cattle barn when they met Mrs. Wiley. She pointed to a blue ribbon rosette the size of a pie pan pinned to her bosom. "Look what Epitome won!" Mrs. Wiley was not exactly smiling, but the corners of her mouth weren't turned down. Her black eyes looked more soft than sharp. "Champion Hereford sire. The breaks in the hide took off a few points, but he was first all the same. He's a great animal, and already some of the cattle producers are interested in buying his calves. Maureen, I heard how you kept him from getting worse hurt thrashing around in the fence. I'm much obliged and intend to make it right for you with an appreciation gift."

"Thanks, Mrs. Wiley. I was by myself and thought he might tear up jack when he got loose."

"I'll have to do some considering for something appropriate for you." She touched the rosette. "I'm going to show this to your grandma and the ladies at the church booth. They don't give these for crocheted doilies."

Maureen and Walter went on to the cattle pavilion, and Maureen felt a little pride herself when everyone there admired Epitome. By noon, they had seen all the livestock and were ready for the twenty-five-cent chicken dinner at the church booth.

After dinner, they looked at the needlework and canned fruit, watched a fellow demonstrate a gadget that cut radishes into roses, and signed for chances to get free rug cleaning. Still, it was quite a while until four o'clock.

Maureen loved the sound of the carrousel music that started in the carnival section of the fair. "I don't feel abased, Walter. I feel more like abounding." Maureen took long leaps toward the music. Walter caught up with her, and they walked by the wheel-of-fortune booth to the show tent. "I think we did a good thing letting people know about our apple. Even talked up to the judge."

"But Maureen, Epitome broke the tree. There won't be any more of these." Walter took the last apple from his pocket.

"Stop, Walter." Maureen held his hand as he started to take a bite. "Don't eat it. There are about eight seeds in that apple. We'll plant them and get maybe eight apple trees. That apple is the smidgen we need. Put it back in your pocket where Mit won't see it."

Walter jumped when the rasping voice of the show-tent barker began. "Your chance, your only chance to see skill and wonders beyond your imagination." They studied the big, lurid posters in front of the tent as he described the 500-pound lady, the man with a rubber skin, the sword swallower, the fire-eater, snake charmer, the dwarf family, a human covered with scales like a fish. The pitchman promised countless other wonders and curiosities of the animal world.

"We've never been in the show tent," Walter said. "Let's go this year."

The eyes of the fish-scale-covered man glared down from his picture at them. "I don't know, Walter. Some of it might scare you. We'll go in on one condition. You'll have to keep your eyes shut. I'll describe to you what I see."

Maureen bought two tickets and led Walter into the tent. To give him an idea of the size of the fat lady, she estimated it would take thirty-seven yards of cloth to make her a plain dress. She was relieved that Walter was spared the sight of the man who stretched the skin of his neck and cheeks out as if it were a piece of inner tube. Maureen led Walter on to a pretty woman's stand and was startled when she realized her necklace was a little live snake. She stroked two big ones in her lap like pets.

There were some strange-looking things in big jars of murky liquid that Maureen only glanced at. She didn't want to get sick and lose her chicken dinner. However, she did push through the crowd to get a better view of the cow with two udders.

The last sight was the fish-scale man, who told the crowd he had been born with flaky skin for which there was no cure. With fishy eyes, he looked right at Maureen and peeled off pieces of skin as big as her thumb. As she turned to guide Walter out of the tent, she saw the glint of his eyes through half-closed lids.

"Maureen, you didn't tell me how people can swallow knives and eat fire," he said.

"I don't have to, Walter. Figure it out for yourself. You cheated and opened your eyes."

They strolled on and were surprised to find Mit with his pitching arm drawn back, ready to throw at a pyramid of battered wooden milk bottles. "Mit," Maureen shouted. "We're ready at four o'clock, like you said."

He turned in disgust. "You almost made me miss my last throw."

She moved near him. "Remember, you were going to save every red cent you made."

"Three throws for a dime. I've knocked them down twice. I'm making this last one count." He took careful aim. The stack of bottles collapsed, and the carnival man took a Kewpie doll from the shelf and gave it to Mit.

"Okay, let's go." Mit tried to tuck the doll under his arm, but so many heads turned that he was embarrassed. "Here, you carry it." He shoved it toward Maureen.

She didn't think much of the plaster Kewpie. It had a fat belly, silly grin, pointed head, and bumps like wings on its shoulders. The purple feathers glued around its head and waist were its only clothes. Worse yet, its legs were molded together so that it would be hard to make it proper underwear. But since Mit doubtless intended to give her the Kewpie, she didn't want to belittle his gift by pointing out its defects.

Mr. Stackhouse was in a good humor driving home. He was giving the value of the two blue and three red ribbons his pigs had won when Walter spoke up. "You could get a lot of money for that unicorn. Sell it to the show-tent people."

"What say? What's that?" Mr. Stackhouse asked over the noise of the truck motor.

"Be quiet, Walter." Maureen shook his arm. "Can't you see that Mr. Stackhouse is driving?"

Hazel was waiting on the porch when they pulled up at the store. Maureen wanted to stop to tell her about the fair, but Mit insisted they start their walk home immediately. As soon as they were out of sight of the store, he took the Kewpie from Maureen and straightened its feathered skirt.

That evening Walter was so tired that he went upstairs to bed without urging right after supper. He fell asleep at once, but he didn't stay asleep. Maureen was telling how she got down to her last apple when he called out that knives were being thrown at him. Maureen raced upstairs and quieted him. The second time he cried out, Mama herself went upstairs. When she finally came down, she sat on the edge of a straight chair instead of settling into her rocker.

Mama put her hands on her lips. "Maureen, do you have any idea why Walter is having bad dreams about a man covered with fish scales?"

Maureen tried to look thoughtful. "Say, do you suppose Walter got a glimpse of Old Whisker? Saw it out on the creek bank maybe and too scared to tell us?"

"No, I don't. I think you spent good money to go to the freak show."

"Mama, do you know what Mit did? He spent good money to win a Kewpie doll without enough clothes to dust a fiddle. You won't like it if he gives it to you."

Mama waved her hand as if brushing aside the comments. "I want to know why you went in that tent to stare at freaks?"

"Well, I figured it would be educational."

"Educational!" Mama exclaimed.

"And it was too," Maureen continued. "Now you take a cow with two bags. Might give twice as much milk. Make twice as much butter. Do you think so, Dad?"

"Maureen," Mama snapped. "We're not talking about a cow with an extra, fake, rubber udder tied on."

"Oh, I know, because there were lots of other things," Maureen rushed on. "It was something like Scripture, you know: People shouldn't hide their lights under a bushel. Do you think that means a bushel basket?" She didn't wait for an answer. "Being a freak is just about a full-time job. They have to keep eating away to stay at 500 pounds, make sure skin stays rubbery, practice eating fire. I figured it was all educational, especially for Walter. Freaks have to make a living the same as anybody else. But educational as it was, once is enough. We won't need to go again."

Dad laughed and slapped his leg. "Maureen, you've got a bigger spiel than the show barker."

Maureen began to chant, "All for a dime, ten cents, that will neither make you, break you, buy a farm, or set you up in business."

Mama was smiling a little too and moved to her rocker.

10

Maureen showed Walter the plump, brown seeds in the palm of her hand. "Seven seeds, that's all. We've got to be careful when we plant these."

She explained to him that things sometimes grew in the fall if Indian summer was long and mild. They could plant three seeds at once and save four to plant in the spring. In the trash pile, they found a saucepan with drain holes already rusted in the bottom. They filled it with rich dirt from the barn lot and planted three seeds. A sunny spot by the yard gate was a good place for the pan. They'd see it as they passed and remember to water it.

Maureen kept an eye on Walter so he wouldn't overdo the watering. He was impatient and wanted to dig down and inspect a seed to see if anything was happening. Maureen wouldn't allow it.

Near suppertime one evening, they went to look at the pan and found a little white loop poking out of the ground. It wasn't a weed; an apple seed had sprouted.

"Walter, you don't have to stay out here and guard it. It'll take care of itself. Don't you dig down to see about the other two when I go help Mama with supper, soon as Mit comes."

They heard horse hoofs scraping on the rocks of the lane. The sound wasn't galloping, just the steady plod of a walk. Mit rode old Patsy bareback up to the yard gate. A big smile shone on his face that was dark with dust from the day's work.

"Hey, Maureen! Walter! We are now a one horse farm. Mama! Dad!" he shouted, as he slid off the mare's sway-back. They heard him and came with questioning looks to the gate. "I got us some horsepower," Mit announced. "I never thought I'd get it this way, but you never know."

"What do you mean, Mit?" Dad didn't sound so pleased.

"I figured I'd work and save and someday get us a team of mules. That was my aim. I've cut it down some. The best I can do is come riding home on this mare." Mit laughed as if he'd heard a good joke on the radio. "She's my pay. Mr. Stackhouse gave her to me for my work."

Dad looked shocked. "Didn't he give you cash to boot or knock anything off the store bill?"

"No, but I don't have to give him anything extra. She's free and clear. You'll have yourself a saddle horse, Mama. She's an easy rider. She'll carry double so Maureen and Walter can ride her."

"Well, I declare." Mama, too, was taken aback. She ran

her hand over Patsy's side, which was ridged like a washboard.

"She's a little thin," Mit allowed. "We can fatten her up."

"What with? Did Sterling Stackhouse throw a load of corn into the deal?" Dad sounded angry.

"No, but we can keep this good bridle." Mit pulled at the cheek strap to show its strength.

Dad shook his head. "If we had a crib full of corn, Patsy hasn't got a mouth full of teeth to eat it. She's got a lot of age on her. You realize that, Mit?"

"Oh, sure, Dad, but Mr. Stackhouse said she has a lot of good years left. She comes from real good stock, and she's had time to learn a lot. Patsy is harness-broken for a wagon. Even a plow. She's been a brood mare. She took a ribbon once at Beaumont Fair."

"That must have been a while back." Dad felt Patsy's knee. "She's not worth wintering, Mit. Sterling Stackhouse knows it. That's why he gave her to you. He should have given you a couple of shells to shoot her. You did all your hard work for nothing. He got a lot of free labor out of you."

"Oh, Cleve, not so hard," Mama implored.

"When are you going to get some judgment?" Dad kept on. "I know you can't get ahead of a Stackhouse, but I didn't think he'd take advantage of you on your first job. If we didn't owe such a store bill, I'd take this nag back and collect the cash due Mit."

"It's done now, Cleve." Mama sighed. "Put Patsy in the pasture and come on in to supper."

"Eats for now, but I don't know how the old mare and all the rest of us are going to get through the winter," Dad said.

Mit looked dejected as he led Patsy away. He didn't seem like the same brother who had ridden home in such high spirits.

At supper Dad said nothing. Maureen knew from the look on his face that he might not speak to them again for days. Mit didn't talk and didn't eat, either. Mama looked worried, and Walter's eyes were sad as a hound's.

Maureen tried to make the meal more cheerful. "I think it's just dandy we've got our own horse. We're going to learn to ride her. Ride out to check on our range pigs, won't we, Walter? We'll ride over to visit Sansoucies. Get the one-horse spring wagon out of the barn and hitch up." Maureen held imaginary reins. "We can haul stuff to Uncle Millard's. No more packing everything over there."

"That's enough, Maureen," Mama warned.

"You can drive to the store. *Clip-clap, clip-clap.*" Maureen pounded on the table. "Come spring, we'll hitch Patsy to the plow and rip out the Johnson grass in our bottom field. Get a good stand of corn."

She started to get up to demonstrate holding the plow. Dad drew back his hand, threatening to slap. Maureen dodged and stayed at her place. Only Walter appreciated her efforts. His eyes no longer looked sad.

When Maureen helped with dishes, she saved Mit's supper in case he got hungry before bedtime. She hadn't thought she would ever feel sorry for him, but she did as she looked at him sitting on the back step with his head hung down almost to his knees. His hair was a mess.

She went out and sat beside him. "You never can tell about a horse, especially Patsy. Not everybody knows how special she is. Mr. Stackhouse will be sorry he let her go."

"I never do anything right," Mit said bitterly.

"Oh, sure you do, Mit. Every now and then you do something right. Anyhow, you take a mare like Patsy—"

"Shut up your blather and let me alone." Mit pulled away.

Later Maureen decided that Mit's misery must have lifted some, for he cleaned up his supper plate. The next morning he was up early currying Patsy.

Before Mama could give Maureen enough Saturday jobs for a full week, Maureen wanted to slip off to Uncle Millard's. She'd inform them of McCrackens' horse and tell them to expect her and Walter to come horseback in the future.

It was still as Sunday at Uncle Millard's. There was no squabbling among the little cousins, who were digging in the yard. Oren and Uncle Millard sat on the porch reading Wiley books. Even in the morning Aunt Cora was sitting down with her embroidery hoop. Dessie wasn't doing anything.

Skeets had drawn with chalk all over the porch steps. "Hi, Maureen. Do you and Walter want to play hopscotch? I can make squares here on the porch, almost as good as on a sidewalk."

Hopscotch was a town game new to Maureen. Skeets

was doubtless a whiz at it. "Huh-uh. I've got to save my shoes and can't stay long anyhow. I have to get back and take care of stock."

"Have you seen anything wonderful around here to tell us about?" Dessie asked.

"No, I haven't seen any palaces, no church made out of rock lace," Maureen retorted.

"We've got a horse," Walter announced.

"Are you sure it's not a unicorn?" Skeets bent over her sketch.

Maureen decided to say no more about Patsy. "You took that chalk from school, Skeets. You'd better not let Mrs. Nolen know you stole it."

Skeets shrugged. "I asked her. It's just a little piece, almost used up now. I wish I had more. Look here, Walter. Want to see how to draw a box so it won't look flat?"

Skeets held the bit of chalk in her fingertips and drew a square on the porch floor. She overlapped a second square at the lower right corner of the first. Then she connected the corners of the squares with four straight lines. A cube emerged.

Maureen tried not to show her wonder at the drawing and went over to Uncle Millard's rickety chair. He closed his book over his thumb to show Maureen the cover. "I never read a book like this before. *Walden* by Henry David Thoreau. Did you ever hear of him?"

"The eighth grade hasn't gotten to him yet." Maureen spoke up so that Uncle Millard could hear.

"He's a comfort. Like he says, you don't need near as much in this world as you think you do. Take time to

100

look around. On a walk in the woods, a person might get an idea worth a day's work."

"This Thoreau, was he a family man?" Aunt Cora shouted.

"No, a bachelor," Uncle Millard said, and went on with his reading.

Maureen watched Aunt Cora's needle whip around and form a flower. "This is lazy daisy stitch," she explained. "I just dearly love to do it. See these pretty colors lie down nice and flat to make flower petals. Vido's doing the housework so I can embroider these pillow slips. Dessie is going to sell chances on them for a raffle. She misses the city, you know. Says there's nothing to do here." Aunt Cora threaded her needle. "I keep busy even if we are living at the back of a ditch."

Maureen was indignant. That was no way to talk about the rent-free Wiley place, complete with library. She didn't intend to stay and waste any more of her Saturday. Walter could hang around and draw boxes or Jiggs and Maggie or whatever Skeets was teaching him from the funny papers, but she was going home.

Since she was no longer wary of Epitome, she took the shortest way through the Wiley pasture, the McCracken hayfield, directly to the garden where Mama was digging late potatoes.

Mama had pretty hands, but now they were so dirty her gold wedding ring hardly shone. Maureen started picking up potatoes. "I can't do a thing with Walter, Mama. I left him over there loafing with the rest of them. Skeets is showing off with some stolen chalk. The little kids are digging up the Easter bell bulbs. Aunt Cora is not looking the way you do. She's all washed and combed sitting in the sun doing lazy daisy. Uncle Millard's not climbing around on a high bridge getting spattered with paint like Dad is. He's reading a book by Henry David somebody."

"Thoreau. Must be nice." Mama brought up a hill of potatoes. "I haven't had time to read all summer. My stories in *Capper's Weekly* are piling up."

"Did you ever read that Thoreau book?"

"I started it. Near as I can tell, Thoreau never did a full day's work in his life." Mama put her hand on her back as she straightened up. "Millard and Oren will feed stock for Mrs. Wiley this winter, and she'll help some with Millard's store bill. She's doing a lot for Millard. They'll come out as well as we do. Cora thinks it's Providence. Like Scripture says: The fellow that comes to work at the eleventh hour, near quitting time, gets the same pay as the fellow that works all day."

Maureen was pleased that Mama was talking to her like a Sunday-school teacher. "If that wasn't Scripture, I'd say it wasn't fair. Mama, I hate to tell you this, but Aunt Cora is cutting up the unbleached muslin you gave her for sheets and making it into pillow slips with fancywork for a raffle. I think you should quit digging potatoes and go right over there and put a stop to it."

"Lots of things at the Wiley place don't suit me so well," Mama confided. "When the kids marked the wallpaper, I could have bawled like a cow with a weaned calf. But when you give somebody something, you have to let go of it. Let them handle it."

Damp soil had dried to grit on Maureen's hands. She rubbed them on her dress. "Do you ever feel like everybody else is smarter and prettier and has it easier than you do, Mama?"

"Well, sometimes, and I know who's making me feel that way. That old green-eyed monster, jealousy. He crops up bigger than these spuds."

"Does he get after you, too, Mama? Do you still have to fight him off?"

"Now and then," Mama admitted.

Maureen felt better to know that even Mama sometimes felt sorry for herself.

11

When they came home from school, Walter and Maureen inspected their pan of apple seeds. "Two more. All three came up, Walter. Our seeds sprouted 100 percent."

"How can it be 100 when we only have three sprouts?" Walter asked.

Maureen stood up and brushed dirt from the knees of her stockings. "You'll learn about that in sixth grade, or you can catch on sooner if you listen to my arithmetic class instead of drawing boxes."

Walter whistled some notes, then stopped to beam. " 'Turkey in the Straw.' Just like Dad's whistling."

"Thanks for telling me." Maureen danced a few steps. "I thought it was nothing at all. I'm glad to hear Dad whistle. He's over being so mad about Patsy. I'll beat you to the porch to see what he's doing."

The extra gang's fall work was done, so Dad was home where Maureen could watch him do jobs around the place. She learned all sorts of things that way. Beside Dad's stool was a pile of whips cut from apple trees. Water dripped from the roots of a little sprout that Maureen took out of the bucket beside his feet.

"Grafting, that's what you're doing, huh, Dad? I remember from last year," Maureen said.

"You betcha. I'll add one and one and get one."

"Add one and one, get two," Walter corrected.

Dad examined a whip. "In grafting, you add one and one and get one better."

"Oren's class had this poem. It said, 'only God can make a tree,' but you can make a new one, can't you, Dad?" Maureen asked.

"Oh, no, it's still up to God and nature. I work along," Dad said. "That's the way most things get done."

Maureen asked Dad how he'd learned to graft fruit trees, and he told her he'd just picked it up along the way. She wanted to know how grafting worked.

"It's the darndest thing. It seems everything wants to grow if it has half a chance." Dad took a sprout from the bucket. "This Ben Davis variety is tough as a pine knot."

"And loses all its flavor in storage," Mama said, as she came out of the house with a big clothes basket to take wash off the line.

"So we'll try to graft a variety you like better and get the trees started to grow this fall." Dad stroked his pocket-knife on a whetstone until it was razor sharp. Then, with one clean stroke of the knife, he cut the sprout in two and

105

tossed the top aside. "We'll keep this root. Now we'll take one of these scions from a Winesap tree. That's a good-flavored keeper." Dad selected a whip from the pile.

"Scion? Just a leg-switchin' stick." Maureen brandished one of the whips at Walter's legs. "How come it's a scion?"

"Finer use, finer name," Mama said.

"Still just a little switch. Not even any roots." Dad cut the end of it at the same slanting angle as he had cut the rootstock. "But given a chance, this scion will catch and grow like you and Walter and all Millard's kids."

"I still don't see how it works," Maureen said.

"You have to be very careful to match the cambium layer of the rootstock and the cambium layer of the scion." Dad followed his own directions and placed the angled cuts together. "That cambium layer is between the bark and the woody stem. It doesn't look like much, but it's the lifeline of the plant." Dad wound waxed twine around the joint and tied it carefully. "This makes a good splice graft. It should grow like sixty."

Walter lightly touched the joint. "If you want an apple tree, why don't you plant an apple seed, same as you do for a sunflower or a cucumber or anything else?"

"Apples don't breed true. I know that from experience." Mama put the clothes basket on the step and sat down beside it. "One Christmas when I was about Maureen's age, my present was a book, *Hans Brinker and the Silver Skates*. I curled up in a big chair with my book and the apple I'd found in the toe of my Christmas stocking. It was a good book and a good apple. What kind, I'll never know. I ate it, core and all, everything but the seeds.

There was a Boston fern on a plant stand beside my chair, so I pushed the seeds into the soil around that fern.

"Sure enough, one sprouted and thrived. Soon as the ground thawed that spring, I transplanted it outside. I took care of my apple tree for years. Finally it bloomed, and in the fall it bore three apples. They were sour as quinces and hard as rocks. Good ammunition for a green apple battle. That's how I know apple seeds don't breed true."

Maureen felt a crush of disappointment. "Are you sure? What about that wonderful apple tree we found that grew all by itself?"

"That was chance. Nature comes up with surprises sometimes." Dad covered the roots of the grafted tree with a piece of damp burlap.

"I think nature is downright contrary," Maureen said, "making seeds you can't depend on."

"You have to work along with her," Dad said. "Plant orchards at the top of a chilly north slope that the sun doesn't hit in the spring. Then the flower buds don't open to get nipped by a late freeze. Cold air flows down, so it seldom gets too cold at the top."

"I'll bet mine would have been hard to freeze," Maureen said.

Walter followed her to the oak tree where she slumped in the tire swing. "Maureen, we might as well dump out our pan of apple sprouts."

"I guess so," she agreed.

Walter pushed the swing. "I told Skeets we had these magic apple seeds and that we were going to have wonderful apple trees."

Maureen straightened up and braced her feet to give herself a firm push. "You don't need to tell her any different, because I'm not going to give up."

"I am." Walter went to the gate and turned the pan of seeds upside down. He didn't seem to care one whit and went off trying to whistle "Turkey in the Straw."

From the swing, Maureen watched Mit come up from the bottom field where he had cut and piled dry, coarse Johnson grass for Patsy's winter feed. Mr. Stackhouse had no more work for him; he seldom saw Hazel. At times, he was touchy as a boil. As he came through the gate, he kicked at the mound of dirt. "What's this mess?"

"It's dirt now," Maureen explained, as she slid out of the swing. "Before that, it was a sort of apple plantation." She picked up the leaky pan. "Might as well put this back in the trash pile, because we found out seeds from our wild apple tree wouldn't grow into the same good trees."

"Anybody knows that," Mit said. "How could you live around here and not know it? I'll bet Skeets knows that."

So Mit didn't care one whit about her loss, either. "You think you know everything, but you don't," she asserted. "You don't know that Johnson grass hay is no good. Dad says you're working for nothing again, because Johnson grass is no better than a snowball for wintering stock."

Maureen jumped back, for Mit looked angry enough to fight. He glared at her. "That's not so. You're making that up, Reen Peen."

"I am not, and don't you call me Reen Peen." He hadn't called her the hated nickname for a long time. If their cousins ever heard the name, she'd be stuck with it.

108

"It's a free country, free speech. Anybody is allowed to say Reen Peen, Reen Peen," Mit teased.

"Shut up, Mit!" Maureen yelled.

"Reen Peen, Reen Peen, thought she'd be the apple queen," Mit chanted.

If she hit him with all her might, she still wouldn't hurt him, and he could hit back harder than she could.

"Reen Peen, Reen Peen, thought she'd be the apple queen." Mit was pleased with his rhyme and started it again in a low singsong. "Reen Peen, Reen Peen."

"You shut your big mouth," she shouted.

"Stop tormenting her, Mit, and Maureen, that's enough out of you," Mama called from the porch, where she was sorting laundry. "They'll hear you clear over at Millard's. I declare, Mit comes home, and in no time the two of you have started a ruckus."

"He's the one started it," Maureen protested. "Claims I'm dumb, and—"

"I've got a good supply of little whips here handy, Maureen," Dad said. "Didn't you hear your mother?"

Maureen fled out the gate, up toward the ridge field. None of them cared about anything. Maureen wanted to get away from all of them. She ran until she was out of breath. Then she walked toward McCrackens' woods.

Overhead she heard faint sounds like yapping dogs and looked up to see the wavering V of wild geese flying south. Ahead, the hickory trees stood out in the woods like columns of gold. In spite of herself, she began to enjoy her walk. She remembered how she had run this same way to cut Epitome out of the fence. There was the sassafras tree, the honey locust, and the broken trunk of the wild apple tree between.

Wood ants had started to work in the splintered trunk. Maureen shook dry leaves from the top that hung to the ground. Then she examined the jagged break in the trunk. On the underside of the break, the top was still attached to the trunk by about an inch of bark. Beneath that bark was a strip of cambium layer. Leaves clinging to the branch nearest the strip of bark were not as dry as the rest, and the twigs on that branch had a feel of life. Its fruit spurs and leaf buds were not shriveled.

Maureen needed a sharp knife like Dad's, but it was getting dusk. If she rescued scions that day, she'd have to risk breaking them off and hope for good cuts when she got home.

When she started back across the open field, she looked up at the evening sky and made a double wish on the first star. She wished she'd take a real liking to Skeets and that the apple cuttings would live.

Dad was putting away his grafting equipment when she came waving her apple switches. "Wait, Dad, I want to graft these from my wild tree. I think I've picked up how to do it."

Dad studied the switches and tossed one away. "I think these others are alive. They're skimpy, but you can try them since you set such a store by that tree. If it's as good as everyone claims, it's worth a try to save this stock. A damaged tree like that will die completely over the winter," Dad said.

Walter watched Maureen work carefully with Dad's

sharp knife. She matched cambium layer of the scion with common rootstock and tied the splice firmly with waxed string that would not cut the bark. She didn't nick her finger until she was finished and closed the blade. It was only a slight cut, and she kept Dad from seeing it.

"It takes patience to grow fruit trees," he said. "You won't have apples next summer, and if one of these grafts lives, you'll be lucky."

"Oh, I know. Walter and I will help you take care of them," Maureen promised. "When they're planted, we'll put wire cages around the trunks so the rabbits can't get at them and kill them."

That night when she went to bed, Maureen imagined four beautiful trees just loaded with the world's greatest apples. She thought Walter had been asleep for a long time and was surprised when he called out.

She jumped out of bed and ran to his room. "What is it, Walter, freaks again?"

"No, but I wondered if your finger hurts."

"Not now."

"It's a good thing you didn't give up on our apple," he said.

"It's just what I told you. All you need is a smidgen. Just a smidgen of a cambium layer."

12

Every evening after school Maureen and Walter went to the orchard to see Maureen's grafted trees. Days were getting shorter, and chores had to be done early. Maureen showed Walter a twig on the grafted tree. "See how pink that is? It's alive for sure, almost as pink as the sunset."

They saw Mama going about evening chores and went to help her. In the chicken house, they gathered eggs while she carefully measured out corn for the hens.

"Only five eggs today." Walter showed Mama the round-bottomed basket.

"The hens don't lay so well in cold weather, but they wouldn't be so skimpy with eggs if I wasn't so skimpy with feed." Mama scattered shelled corn. "This stuff is about like gold, color and all."

"I was stone-still when Dad listened to the radio livestock and commodity market. The announcer reported corn was fifty-two cents a bushel."

"Yes, low," Mama agreed, "but since we didn't raise any, we have to put out cash money or manage for it."

Already they had managed to trade Mr. Stackhouse firewood for corn. Occasionally Mit got a day's work from him and was paid two bushels of corn. Maureen wondered if Mit had gotten up the nerve at least to be mannerly to Hazel when he ate at Stackhouses'.

"Once we get our hogs fattened, we'll have more corn for the hens," Mama said. "More for Molly and Patsy, poor old thing. She's got to have grain."

The fussy hens clucked and sang over each grain of corn. Then came squealing from the pigpen. "Dad's feeding hogs, Walter. Let's go watch them eat. I never saw anything wolf down corn the way they do."

As the pigs pushed their heads into the trough, their ragged ears flopped over their little eyes. When they were small, one long slit and two short slits had been cut in each ear to mark them as McCracken pigs ready to be turned out on the free range to root for themselves.

Other years they ranged until they had eaten the mast of acorns from McCracken and Wiley woods. But this fall Maureen herself had heard the fellow on the radio say that mast-fed hogs brought a rock bottom price, while corn-finished hogs could bring top market dollar. Dad had decided to pen the pigs he planned to market and feed them corn for a few weeks. By the marks in their ears, he knew he had rounded up all the McCracken hogs except for a few left to range.

"I'm glad you understand about hogs, Walter," Maureen said. "I tried to tell Skeets about them, and she thought a finished hog was funny and said mast was part of a boat. Then she drew a picture of a hog and put eyelashes on it."

The day came when no more corn could be spared, and the market was up by one-quarter cent. At supper that night, Dad announced he had rented the Stackhouse truck and would head for National Stockyards, Illinois, early in the morning with a load of hogs.

"I can't go, Dad," Mit said. "Mr. Stackhouse has a day's work for me. Wants me to help butcher."

"I was depending on you to go with me, Mit. Stackhouse didn't say anything about needing you when I rented the truck."

"Let me go! Let me go, please!" Maureen got up and went to Dad's chair. "It'll be educational. I can make a special report at school."

"Lillian has her hands full here, and I do need somebody to keep me on the route," Dad said. "There are a lot of streets in Saint Louis. I have to make sure I get the one that goes across the river to Illinois and the stockyards."

It was still dark when Mit and Dad finished loading the truck. Maureen sat in the cab beside Dad and felt in her coat pocket once again to make sure she still had the road map. In the excitement of getting ready, she had misplaced the map twice.

The paved road north of Beaumont was so smooth that Maureen nodded, for she had awakened often in the night to look at the clock. Her head came up with a jerk.

She had been asleep for quite a while. It was broad daylight, and the map showed they had covered many miles. Dad had gotten up early too. She'd better talk to him so he wouldn't fall asleep. It was the best chance she'd had for a long time.

After an hour or so, the highway began to look like one long Main Street. "You've been talking a blue streak, Maureen." Dad stared straight ahead at the highway. "You'll have to stop now. We're getting into city traffic, and I'm a back-road driver. I've got to keep my mind on where I'm going, or we'll have hogs in the wrong place."

"I didn't mean to be a blatherskite, Dad. It's a good thing we are getting here early before all these city people go to work, isn't it? We'll soon have our hogs off this truck. Even in cold weather like this, they'll lose weight if they don't get water. Mit told me that, and we want them to weigh—"

"Maureen, unfold that map to the part showing Saint Louis streets. Make sure I make a right turn off Route 21 to Gravois. That's all I want to hear from you."

Maureen looked up the street. Among the tangle of wires, signs, and traffic signals, she was relieved to see the highway number. "You're still on 21, Dad. I feel like Prince Henry the Navigator. I heard about him listening to Oren's history class. It took some nerve to start out the way he did in a boat. Ever hear of him?"

Dad didn't answer. Maureen studied the small brick homes they were passing and wondered what it would be like to live with a neighbor so close there was hardly room to walk between the houses. They came to a wide street where she saw a huge building spread out like a circus tent.

She wanted to ask Dad what it was, but he had a question for her. "Are we still on 21?"

For four blocks, she scanned the jumble of signs and signals. There was no route marker in sight.

"I think we're off the route," Dad said grimly. "What street is this?"

Maureen located the position of the street sign, but they were by it before she could read it. She looked at her map where names in fine print were also hard to read.

"Prince Henry the Navigator," Dad said with a snort. He turned to the right. "Maybe I can get on it again." The brakes shrieked, and he started to back up. "Maureen, you've got to help me see these one-way streets." He turned onto another street. "Choteau Avenue! What are we doing here?"

Maureen looked out at dilapidated buildings and felt as dejected as the people who sat in their littered doorways.

"We're losing good time," Dad fumed. "I wanted to get there early. That's the best time to sell. I should have brought Skeets. She knows the city and wouldn't have gotten lost."

Maureen felt miserable as she tried to read street signs on posts, then street names on the map. Dad seemed to be driving aimlessly. The map fell to her feet, and she didn't bother to pick it up. Trying to find anything in the maze of endless streets seemed useless. The longer Dad drove, the heavier traffic became, so Maureen knew it was near nine o'clock, when city people went to work. They had lost half an hour or more. Dad had expected to have the hogs sold and be headed home by nine.

"Now everybody is coming at me," Dad said, "coming in to work. If I'm going east, I'm all right, but if I'm going west, I'm driving in a circle."

The truck body swayed as he made a quick right turn. A huge bridge span loomed ahead, and they eased into heavy traffic. An empty stock truck came toward them. They were so high that Maureen was afraid to look down at the Mississippi River.

"You're on it, Dad. Right smack on the bridge." She hoped it was the right one.

Straight streets led over flat land to the stockyards, which were busier than Beaumont Fair on entry day. It seemed like the middle of the day there. Someone waved Dad toward an empty pen. He backed the truck, let down the tailgate, and the hogs ran down to huddle in a corner of the pen. Even winter couldn't freeze up the smells of the stockyards.

"Stay in the truck, Maureen. We'll be lucky if there is a commission man still making offers."

Maureen knew the commission men charged 1 percent to buy, then turned around and charged another 1 percent to sell. They were the middlemen.

She was relieved when two men wearing big, wide-brimmed Stetson hats and sheepskin jackets came stomping through the mire in their high leather boots. She knew they were commission men when they went to the pen and prodded McCrackens' hogs with their sticks. One of the men talked to Dad and wrote something on a slip of paper. Dad stared at it as if he couldn't believe what he read.

The second man prodded at the hogs until they all trotted into another corner of the pen. He was pointing to them and waving his stick as he talked. Dad was talking, too, as the commission man wrote on a slip and handed it to him.

Maureen saw the dark look come over Dad's face. The commission man shook his head and turned away. Maureen heard him say something about "final offer." Dad followed him a few steps, then just stood looking helpless. His offer didn't lift the cloud from Dad's face.

Maureen knew she'd caused Dad trouble, but she wasn't helping him now just sitting in the truck. She jumped down from the high step of the cab and went to the stock pen. "Have we come too late?"

Dad didn't look at her. "The fellow I wanted to do business with is done buying for the day. He might have given me a fair deal. These two offer the lowest price because our hogs are earmarked."

Maureen was puzzled. "Earmarks have nothing to do with pork."

Dad shuffled the penciled slips of paper. "They think the earmarks mean our hogs are right off the range. Fattened on acorns, snakes, and lizards."

"But we fed them corn, good corn."

"So I told them, but they won't believe a fellow up here in the city." Dad pulled the collar of his denim jacket up around his ears. "Stay in the truck like I told you. I'll wait. Maybe get a better offer."

The commission men had gone into a small building near the stock pens. Instead of getting into the truck, Maureen slipped behind it and went to the building herself. It was not a warming shed as she had supposed but a cramped office with muddy floor and ringing telephones. Commission men, all wearing their Stetson hats, worked at high desks that were little more than shelves. Maureen recognized the man who had made the first offer and went to his desk.

Around his neck he wore something that looked like a shoestring held together with a silver bull's head. He had pushed his big hat to the back of his head and was working with figures. Maureen wondered if he was adding up his commissions. He looked at her and grinned. His fat face and little eyes made Maureen think that he'd been around pigs too long and was beginning to look like one. "Are you getting cold out there?" he asked.

Maureen took a deep breath. The time had come to speak up. "No, but I'm getting mad. It burns me up when my dad, Cleve McCracken, says something is so, and somebody that doesn't know him says it's not so. If you lived in Dotzero, you'd know whatever he says is the truth. And if he says our pigs are corn fed, well then, they are. So if he says it here at National Stockyards, Illinois, it's just as true as it is in Dotzero, and it makes me mad for you not to believe him."

The commission man kept at his figures. "Well, we get all kinds coming in here, girlie."

"My name is Maureen McCracken, and our hogs are corn fed, which was not easy considering we didn't raise any corn this year because we didn't have any mules. We had to manage or swap for corn from Sterling P. Stackhouse. That's his truck out there."

"I saw his name and address on it." The commission man kept on figuring. "Dotzero, Missouri. That's down in the Ozarks. We have to watch for those razorback hogs coming up from the hills. We can tell mast-fed range hogs by the earmarks. It's a rule we've got here."

"Down in the Ozarks! That could be just about anywhere," Maureen objected. "Dotzero is in the Saint Francois Mountains. The Ozarks are spread so much that nobody knows where they are for sure."

The commission man stopped his work. "Listen, Miss Maureen, why don't you go out and help your dad?"

"Because I'm helping him in here."

"Why aren't you in school?" he asked.

"Because I'm on this educational trip."

"I'll tell you something for your education. I've got regular customers who buy from me. People that supply meat to fancy restaurants and butcher shops. If I sell them oily, tough, mast-fed pork, I'll lose my good customers. But I guess that's all shoptalk to you. Heh, heh, heh." His laugh sounded like a pig's grunt.

"I already know about that. We heard on the radio that mast-fed hogs were docked, so that's why we rounded ours up and fed them corn. We had to scrimp on corn for the hens, and they fell off laying. Molly, our cow, just about went dry, and we don't know if our mare, Patsy, will make it or not. You never saw anything eat the way those hogs did. So by rights, you ought to pay a better price."

The commission man was annoyed. He scribbled out his figures. "Are you telling me how to run my business?"

"No, but I want to tell you about earmarks, just so you'd know. We marked their ears and let them out on the range to grow and get big enough to fatten. Once their ears are cut, they don't grow back together." Maureen was running out of things to talk about so as to keep the man's attention. "You can't make a silk purse out of a sow's ear. You've heard that. You can't make a whole ear out of a slit ear either." The commission man threw down his pencil.

The little office was hot. Maureen unbuttoned her coat and took off her stocking cap. "One thing we found out. A hog will gain a pound a day if you keep the corn coming."

"How much did you pay for the corn?" The man folded his arms across his chest as if resigned to a long lecture.

"Fifty-two cents a bushel. Only we traded wood for all except some Mit got as pay for working for Mr. Stackhouse. We'll haul the wood soon as Patsy gets used to harness again."

"And what kind of corn did you feed your hogs?"

"Reed's Yellow Dent," Maureen answered without hesitation. "It's the best, and we saved some of the big ears that were filled out to the end of the cob. That's for next spring's seed. We're in hopes of raising some in the bottom field if Patsy lives and is strong enough to whip out the Johnson grass."

The commission man was drawing doodles on his note

pad. "You do seem to know considerable details. Rate of gain, kind of corn. Maybe I ought to have another look at those hogs."

Dad was getting mad again when he couldn't find Maureen and was surprised to see her coming from the office with the commission man.

"I might be able to do a little better," he said. "Miss Maureen here has talked me into it." After more prodding and study of the hogs, he gave his second offer. "Here you are. Top of the market. Reweigh your truck, and I'll get your check ready."

When Dad took the check, he just sat there in the cab looking at it. "Now that's more like it. Quite a percentage of difference." He didn't start the motor until a trucker behind honked twice for him to move off the scale. Even then he took his time putting the check into his wallet.

At a red light, Dad glanced at Maureen. "You beat all, Maureen, talking up to that shrewd middleman. You know what you did? You saved our corn."

"They made me mad, not believing you, so I thought it was better to speak up than to stay mad all day." She unfolded her map. "We got here, so it ought to be easy to get back. I'll pay attention."

Dad seemed confident about driving. "The day's yet young. Anything you want to do here in the city, Maureen?"

"Uncle Millard's kids say there is a picture show here, Loews State, that's a regular palace. I'd like to see it."

"Once across the bridge, we'll be in downtown Saint

Louis," Dad said. "We can find a lot to park the truck, get washed up, have a bite to eat, ask directions to the theater, and take in the show."

"Won't that cost a lot?"

"Whatever it is, I figure it's your commission." Dad began to whistle as he drove.

Everything went as Dad had planned, and they were at the ticket booth for the first matinee. They entered a white marble room big enough to hold McCrackens' house, dormer windows and all. Little angels peeked out from pink clouds painted on the ceiling. Maureen's worn patent-leather slippers sank into the thick red carpet. A red-and-gold parrot greeted them from its perch as they went up the wide marble stair.

The second room was more beautiful than the first, with walls of blue velvet. Maureen was dazzled by blue, red, and purple light shining through glass fruit in golden bowls on high, carved stands. She didn't know if she was trembling from her own excitement or from the vibration of the organ music.

In the third room, they sat down in cushioned seats just as the enormous red curtain with gold fringe rose. Then a silk curtain turned yellow, violet, green, before it flowed aside. A pink cord caught up the last flimsy curtain so they could watch Shirley Temple tap-dance with her curls bouncing.

The place was a palace, all right, no doubt about it! Maureen wished Walter were there. She wasn't sure she could make him believe how beautiful it was.

13

Mama, Walter, and Mit listened closely as Dad told of the two low-price offers he had received. He had been ready to head for home with no cash and more hogs than they could winter. Maureen had disappeared, and he was so outdone with her that he was ready to leave her at the stockyards. That was Maureen's cue to tell what had gone on in the little office. Then as Dad finished reporting the top-price sale, Mama just beamed at Maureen. She approved the cost of the movie-palace tickets as Maureen's commission.

Mama got out her tablet and figured there was enough cash to pay some on the store bill and to buy shoes for Maureen and Walter. She was ready to figure in high boots for Mit, but he wouldn't hear of it. He had opossum hides to sell and said he'd manage for his own clothes. Mama put some cash aside in case they needed a doctor and for Christmas.

At school, Maureen frequently reported on her Saint Louis trip. She especially liked repeating it to Walter, for then she included the splendors of the movie palace.

"Are you going to tell Skeets and Oren and all of them about going to a palace?" Walter asked one day, when he and Maureen were gathering hickory nuts. "You remember you said there wasn't any such thing except in stories about fairies and kings and queens."

"I know what I said. It's one of those things you can't believe until you see it. I'll tell them," she assured him.

"When?"

Maureen hefted the bag of nuts they had gathered. "We won't find any more nuts this year. If you're going to pester the life out of me, we'll go tell them right now."

At the Wiley place, Vido had just mopped the linoleum. Maureen tiptoed around its edge to the sitting room, which was an awful mess. Snippets of cloth, paper patterns, scraps of yarn littered the room. Aunt Cora sat in the midst of it with her embroidery hoop as if she had nothing to do but fancywork. Dessie was embroidering, too, and Skeets was drawing on unbleached muslin.

It wasn't easy for Maureen to admit she'd been wrong about the movie palace. She didn't know whether to blurt the story out or to ease into it. "What's going on?" she asked.

Aunt Cora shifted her hoop. "Making dolls. Last year I sold a few around Christmas to a shop in Saint Louis."

"Too bad you didn't have them done when I went there

on the stock truck," Maureen said. "I could have sold them for you. I helped Dad sell our corn-fed hogs."

Skeets sketched features on a circle of cloth. "We know. You told it umpteen times at school."

"Not all of it." Maureen launched into her story. She ended with a description of Loews State Theater. "So it was like you said, a palace. That place just made me shiver."

"Now I guess you'll believe something," Dessie said.

"Believe! Why I believe all sorts of things," Maureen declared.

"Well, nothing reasonable." Maureen thought she saw Dessie wink at Skeets.

"We didn't sell all the hogs." Maureen picked up scraps of cloth. "You can come help when we butcher. We have to grind sausage, render lard, start curing hams with hickory-flavored salt."

"I'll speak to Millard about it," Aunt Cora said. "I'm not much of a hand at butchering. I'd like to get a supply of these dolls made. I thought Mrs. Stackhouse might take some to sell at the Dotzero store."

Maureen looked at a stuffed doll's body. "I don't mean to throw cold water, Aunt Cora, but I never saw a rag doll in a store."

"Handmade, not rag." Aunt Cora pinned a pattern to new fabric. She didn't place the pattern and cut to save cloth as carefully as Mama would have done.

Dessie selected a piece of printed cotton for a doll's dress. "I wish it didn't take any more goods than this for me. I sure would like to have a new dress."

126

Aunt Cora looked at the faces Skeets had drawn. "I knew you'd make them nice. That's what you need to catch the eye these days in the toy line. Do you want to help with the embroidery, Maureen?"

Maureen wasn't going to admit that she didn't know how to embroider. She could cook. At McCrackens' that seemed more important. She watched Aunt Cora's needle whip around to form big brown eyes. Two tiny dots made a nose. Short-and-long red stitches became a rosebud mouth. Learning to embroider might be fun.

Aunt Cora handed Maureen a circle of marked muslin stretched taut in embroidery hoops. First thing, the six-strand embroidery thread snarled. Aunt Cora showed her how to give it a tug to pull out the knot. Maureen dreaded to start again and wished she could escape to the sunny outdoors and crack nuts with Walter and the little kids.

Aunt Cora demonstrated the outline stitch. "Now you take a stitch, come up in the middle of it, needle down just beyond, come up again at the end of the first stitch."

"Oh, I see," Maureen said, but she didn't really see. Her needle didn't behave like Aunt Cora's or even like Dessie's. The curves she tried to embroider for eye ovals flattened to straight lines.

Skeets handed her three more pieces of muslin with sketched faces. "That doesn't look like my pattern. What happened to the eyes? That doll will look like it's asleep."

"That's what I meant it to be." Maureen was positive. "Something different, like Aunt Cora said. I want this to be a sleeping doll."

"I'm finished." Skeets sent scraps flying as she cartwheeled across the room, came down with her feet against the wall, got her balance, and stood on her head. From the dirty spot on the wallpaper, Maureen could tell it was a place of frequent headstands.

Dessie started to rip out Maureen's work when Aunt Cora stopped her. "Maybe Maureen has an idea here. We could put two faces together. Awake on one side. Turn it over, and it's asleep. We could make dresses with butterfly sleeves, the same front and back. Yarn hair along the head seam at the top with braids down each side would work either way. So, Maureen, it looks as if you came up with something that will catch on."

Aunt Cora started to put a sleep-awake doll together. She called to Vido to peel potatoes for dinner, because she didn't want to stop sewing. "Here, Dessie," she said, "sew these underpants. Remember you do the middle seams first, sides second, crotch last."

Maureen embroidered three more sleep faces. She offered to go with Aunt Cora when she tried to sell dolls at Stackhouses' store.

On the day set, Maureen met Aunt Cora at the store after school. They showed Mrs. Stackhouse the novel design and urged her to inspect the needlework. Hazel jiggled one of the dolls in a dance on the counter, but Mrs. Stackhouse appeared afraid to touch it for fear it would stick to her. Although Maureen thought they had only a 3-percent chance of selling, she tried her best to talk Mrs. Stackhouse into buying some dolls wholesale. Finally Mrs. Stackhouse said they had to watch what they put their money into. Toys were about the last thing people bought. Then Mr. Stackhouse came to the dry-goods counter of the store, and he was no help. He said people expected store-bought things to be made in a factory.

When Mr. and Mrs. Stackhouse went to weigh sugar and whole coffee for a customer, Hazel confided to Maureen. "If I had my say-so, we would have taken them. I think they would sell for sure."

"Sure as beans on washday," Maureen agreed.

Maureen thought Aunt Cora would be all out of heart when Stackhouses didn't take any dolls, not even one in trade, to lower their store bill. "Pay no attention to Stackhouses, Aunt Cora," Maureen said. "I know you must feel about like I did when they wouldn't let me put my apples in the fair to win the prize. Learn how to be abased and how to abound, like you said."

Aunt Cora smiled as if she didn't mind not having all her teeth. "Oh, I know. Paul to the Romans said 'abound in hope.' That's what I do." Maureen wondered what hope there could be, considering there was only one store in Dotzero.

Just as they were leaving the store, Mrs. Nolen came down the school hill carrying a stack of school papers and her empty lunch box.

Maureen showed her a doll. "Look at this, Mrs. Nolen, handmade, just as nice as you please because Aunt Cora is a good sewer. Ought to be factory made, Mr. Stackhouse claims, and they wouldn't take any for the store. Kids would have a lot of fun with these awake-asleep dolls."

Mrs. Nolen was interested. "Could I borrow one of them

for a few days? I'd like to show it to the WPA sewing-room coordinator. She's due here this week. You know we finally got our project approved so we can have work for women."

All during the next week, Maureen kept still and didn't pester Mrs. Nolen about the doll, although she wondered what had happened to it. One evening when she and Walter came home from school, it was on the kitchen table, awake side up.

"Aunt Cora left that for you, Maureen," Mama said. "The WPA sewing-room lady was really taken with that doll. It did the trick. Aunt Cora got herself a job, ten hours a week, supervising at the sewing room. She's even happier than she was trimming hats."

Maureen turned the doll from one side to the other. "I didn't know they would make anything that was fun. I guess this is my commission."

"They have lots of surplus cotton for stuffing, according to the boss lady. She said they'd need Cora to teach the other women how to make it. As soon as she heard the size of Millard's family and their circumstances, she put Cora on. By Christmas, those dolls will be ready for children that wouldn't have a gift otherwise."

"Aunt Cora abounds in hope," Maureen said.

Mama nodded. "Hope and plans. With her first money, she plans to get herself a peg tooth."

14.

Days were short and cold. Maureen had to remind herself it was regular bedtime and not the middle of the night as she looked out her bedroom window. A curve of pale moon shone over the twiggy top of the oak tree. A few stars sparkled.

There was a closed in, winter quietness about the Mc-Cracken farm. Molly and Patsy were shut in the barn for the night. The chickens had been snug on their roost since early dusk. Tisket didn't whine at the door, for she had been let in to snooze by the stove.

Maureen remembered the double wish she had made on the first star the evening she had cut the apple scions. It seemed to be coming true. The grafts were still alive in the orchard beyond the barn. She couldn't see yellow lamplight from the Wiley place, but she liked to think of

131

Uncle Millard's family over there across the fields. So she must be feeling better about Skeets and all of them. She knew she was feeling good about herself. She'd been a help to both families. Everyone said so, even Mit.

Maureen found it harder to like Skeets at school. She was often ready to tattle to Mrs. Nolen that Skeets was skipping her assignments. Then she would realize it wouldn't do any good.

Mrs. Nolen didn't seem to mind that Skeets used all her time and all the red and green construction paper to make Santas, bells, candles, wreaths. Every time Skeets put another decoration up over the blackboard, Mrs. Nolen stood back and admired it.

Skeets's desk was cluttered with snowflakes and stars ready to decorate the Christmas tree as soon as it was brought through the schoolhouse door. Maureen had all she could do to keep on figuring her percentage problems, for she longed to stop work and start celebrating Christmas.

Finally the day came when Mrs. Nolen gave out parts for the Christmas program. Maureen was pleased not to be assigned a piece to recite. Recitations were for lower grades.

She was sure to have a part in a dialogue. Mrs. Nolen described the first one, which was about Santa's workshop. Maureen begged to be an elf. Mrs. Nolen smiled and said she thought Skeets was more elfin. Walter got to be an elf too, and Oren was Santa. Then came the good part. Maureen was to be Mrs. Claus and boss all the elves while Santa read his mail.

Maureen had her long part memorized for the first practice. Even before they discussed costumes, she had planned to wear Mama's red summer dress. The dress wasn't a bad fit, but Mama said she couldn't wear a short-sleeved dress and take cold.

With arms covered and feet dry, Maureen managed to take cold anyhow just when the others had learned their parts. Mama kept her home for a whole week. They couldn't risk a chance of pneumonia and a doctor's bill.

Mama wouldn't listen when Maureen protested over and over again that having a cold wasn't being sick. Maureen watched her knit Walter a stocking cap for the elf play. It would also be a Christmas present to wear the rest of the winter.

Maureen decided to make Christmas presents too and took slick, colored pages from the old spring-summer Sears catalog. They were the best for catalog beads. She cut the pages into equal-sized triangles. Then she made a cup of smooth flour paste. It would take a lot of beads to make strands for Skeets, Mrs. Nolen, and Grandma.

She coated a triangle with paste, started at the base, rolled it around a toothpick up to the pointed end to form an oblong shape. When the paste was dry, she slid out the toothpick, leaving a hole so the bead could be strung.

The job was messy. She wished she could draw pictures to give people as Skeets did or knit as Mama did.

Late one afternoon Mama took time to show Maureen how to place the right-hand knitting needle under a stitch on the left needle, put the yarn over, and draw the new stitch off to the right needle. As she practiced, Maureen thought she would knit a sweater for Grandma. But her knitting looked odd. Flaws showed up. The shape was wrong, and she took a long time to knit a row.

She wished she could stop knitting and go out with Mama to gather eggs. When Mama opened the door, Tisket ducked in. She trembled as she turned and turned before settling down, like a round, white cushion, for a nap. Short-haired dogs felt the cold. Maureen studied her knitting. It looked about the right size and shape for Tisket. As soon as Mama could show her how to bind the knitting off the needle, she'd have one present done, a sweater for Tisket.

All during the long week at home, Maureen wondered how Walter could get along at school without her and come home whistling every evening. On Friday, she asked him if he was sure he knew his elf part for the play.

"Glue these eyes on this teddy bear," Walter chanted in answer. "I'll start loading up. Don't forget the reindeer hay."

"You don't say that, Walter. You're all mixed up. That's what Skeets says. Your part is 'I'll hurry and put a tail on this hobby horse.'"

"No, Mertie says that. She's an elf now, and I say what Skeets said when she was an elf."

"Couldn't she stop drawing and learn a little part like that? I could say it backwards."

"She learned it all right, but now she's Mrs. Claus."

"She is not!" Maureen jumped up and knocked a jar of Vick's VapoRub off the table beside her. "I'm Mrs. Claus."

Walter fidgeted with the books he had brought home. "When you didn't come to school for a week, Mrs. Nolen said we had to practice our play. Everybody in Dotzero is coming to the program expecting to see something. So she let Skeets be Mrs. Claus because she was there."

"Well, I'm *going* to be there, get my treat, and see the tree." Maureen declared. "Does she think I'm going to die or something? I'd have been there this week if Mama didn't think every puff of wind would blow me away."

"You'll be on the program, Maureen." Walter took a booklet from the bottom of his stack of books. "Mrs. Nolen said you learn fast, and you can say this extra long piece she marked in here."

Maureen snatched the program booklet from Walter and found the poem marked with Mrs. Nolen's good handwriting. She read the verses and threw the book down in disgust. "That's the sappiest piece I ever read. All about leaving a piece of cake for Santa and giving him a present. A bag for toys, la-di-da, and I'm in the sixth grade. I'm not going to say any such piece."

Maureen went into the hall. "Walter, you tell Mama the smell of VapoRub has made me so sick I'm going up to bed. Mit can have my supper."

On her dresser, Maureen had placed the catalog beads to dry. There were enough for one strand, and she wasn't making any more. Mrs. Nolen didn't deserve any. Skeets would turn cartwheels, stand on her head, and strangle herself if she wore any.

Maureen began to think of the Christmas program and

135

had an idea that made her feel better. Below there were sounds of supper making, and she was glad when Walter came up to ask if she was sure she didn't want any.

"I might eat a bite or two when it's ready," she allowed. "Listen, Walter, I've thought of something. If I can't be Mrs. Claus, I'm going to make up my own dialogue."

Walter sat down on the braided rug on the floor beside Maureen. "Who'll be in it?"

"I'll be in it, that's who. I'll be all the parts except the dog. Tisket has that part. She can come to school the day of the program."

Walter's eyes looked big and sad, "Mrs. Nolen won't let you have a dialogue not in the book."

"Sure she will when she hears how good it is. I'll tell you how it will go. First there's this brave girl, Gretchen. Do you like that name?" Walter nodded, and Maureen continued. "Gretchen just sits here knitting and knitting. She knits socks for the whole family. And all they do is wear them out. She no more than gets one pair done than she has to knit up another pair. Gretchen, I'm her."

"Who is she talking to about all that knitting?" Walter inquired.

"Well, she speaks to her faithful dog. The dog's name is Wolverette, because she's like a small wolf. Only it's Tisket.

"Then Gretchen goes out and in comes Hans. That's me, too, in Mit's overalls and cap with earflaps down. He's bellyaching because he's got holes in the heels of his socks. He wants a new pair knit right away. Also he's hungry and wants Gretchen to cook his dinner, only he's talking to the dog."

"Where does Christmas come in?" Walter asked.

"I'm getting to it. Next in comes Fritz, another brother. That's me, too, in Dad's hunting coat. He tells Wolverette he is glad to see that Gretchen has stopped knitting and gone to make Christmas goodies, which is what he wants.

"Then in comes Gretchen's stepmother wearing Mama's long-sleeved dress. She hollers into the cloakroom at Gretchen, who isn't there because I'm her being my own stepmother. She yells at Gretchen to finish knitting her lace stockings so she can go to Christmas market day over by the palace. She's alway gadding and leaves all the work to Gretchen."

"It's something like Cinderella," Walter commented.

"It is not, because Cinderella didn't have a dog. And this Gretchen—that's me—has. So she comes back in and says to the dog, 'Everybody around here is driving me nuts, all wanting something except you, Wolverette. B-r-r-r, it's bitter chill. While I had to sit here five hours watching the plum pudding get done, I knit you this red coat.' So then I put this coat on Tisket."

"What if Tisket scratches it off and runs away?" Walter asked.

"I'll get a good grip on her. She's my own dog. Anyhow, it will be the end of the first act, and I'll pull the sheet across on the wire so everybody will know it.

"I come out in front of the curtain for the second act. It's Christmas morning, and Gretchen is calling Wolver-

137

ette, who is lost. She looks down, and there's this piece of red yarn. 'What's this?' she asks herself. By now, everybody will know she's been through enough to talk to herself. 'Why, why, 'tis Wolverette's red coat. She's caught it on a twig, and it has raveled out as she ran. I must follow it to find her.'

"So then I go out the girls' door and come in the boys' door, still following that red string.

"Behind the curtain, I've put a little cedar tree with red applies tied on it, and Tisket is tied to a chair close by, but you can't see she's tied. I pull back the curtain, and I'm dumbfounded to see this tree and Wolverette. I say, 'A tree, with ripe fruit in winter's cold? Why . . . why . . . how amazing! And I was led to this miracle of Christmas by my faithful Wolverette, the one that asked for naught.'

"Then I close the curtain and everyone claps and claps. What do you think of it, Walter?"

"What's naught?"

"That's book talk for nothing."

Walter smiled until his eyes shut. "I hope Mrs. Nolen lets you have that dialogue soon as you're well."

"I'm well now, and I'm going to stay that way and not let anything happen to Tisket either."

Mama called that supper was waiting.

Maureen beat Walter downstairs.

15

In Maureen's opinion, school was a mess. Class time was spent practicing Christmas dialogues in which she had no part. The room was dark, because Skeets had pasted Santa's sleigh and reindeer all over the windows. The kids were wound up. Mrs. Nolen was discombobulated. No matter how many times Maureen asked if she could give her original play, she never got a straight answer. Mrs. Nolen's replies were, "We'll see. I'll get to that later. Don't bother me about that now."

"I can't pin her down," Maureen explained to Walter the evening before the program, "but I'm taking Tisket to school with me tomorrow just in case. Don't you chase off with Uncle Millard's kids. I'll need you to carry my bag of costumes. I've got to take a little cedar tree, a lard bucket to stand it up in, and apples wired ready to put on it."

Getting Tisket to follow along to school the next morning was no problem. Usually she had to be ordered home at the bridge. The cedar sapling that Maureen balanced on her shoulder pricked her neck. The cold wind went right through her mittens and stiffened her fingers. She was glad she and Walter had thick-soled shoes, for the ground was frozen hard.

Tisket whined and pulled at the collar and rope Maureen used to tie her to the school porch. The last bell was ringing, so Maureen and Walter hurried into the warm schoolroom.

Mrs. Nolen was all dressed up in a ruffled white blouse and pleated skirt that whirled when she moved, but she looked worried. "There're always colds and flu going around this time of year," she said, "and I'm sorry it has hit *h*, *m*, and *s*. We can't spell Christmas without those letters, so we'll have to drop that number." She pushed aside on her cluttered desk the stack of big tinfoil-covered letters that Skeets had made for nine little kids to hold up as they said pieces for each letter to spell *C-H-R-I-S-T-M-A-S*. "Maureen, did you say you had something you could do to fill in?"

"Yes, ma'am."

"With some classwork to do, the big tree to trim, and straightening up, we won't have time for another practice. Are you sure you know what you're doing?"

"Yes, Mrs. Nolen. I'm ready."

140

The morning raced by in a confusion of excitement. At one o'clock Hazel came, a whole hour before the program was to start. She slid into the seat beside Maureen. "Is Mit coming?" When Maureen nodded, Hazel beamed. "I was in hopes I'd see him today."

Maureen wondered what it would be like to want to see someone who didn't know how to talk to you. "Do you feel extra happy on the days you see a certain person?" she asked.

Hazel giggled. "Sure do."

Maureen was puzzled. "I don't understand it."

"I don't either," Hazel admitted, "but it might happen to you sometime whether you understand it or not."

Mit came early too with Melvin Stackhouse and looked quickly around the room. Although he let his eyes slide right over Hazel, he knew she was there. Above the reindeer on the window, Maureen saw Mama, Dad, Aunt Cora, Vido, and Uncle Millard carrying Yvonne coming across the playground. She felt like running out to greet them.

Grown-ups squeezed into school seats. The crowd around the wall made a place for the Stackhouses, who were the last to come.

Mrs. Nolen's face was flushed as she stood at the front of the room to welcome visitors. "At the start of our program, I'd like you to know our outstanding decorations were made by Crystal O'Neil, our Skeets, or under her supervision." Mrs. Nolen's skirt twirled as she turned and pointed around the room. "I have to keep teaching, so I

141

just put her in charge. Before she is transformed into Mrs. Claus for one of our dialogues, she'll take a bow."

Maureen didn't see much need to clap too hard, since there was plenty of applause. When things quieted down, she could hear Tisket whining outside to be free.

The little children all got through their recitations without much prompting. In the Santa's workshop dialogue, Walter remembered his part and was the right size and shape for an elf. Skeets was too puny for Mrs. Claus, but the play got a lot of clapping anyhow.

There were more songs, recitations, and dialogues by the upper grades. The room was getting very stuffy. Babies squirmed and fretted. Little children pushed by visitors and stumbled over feet in a parade to the outdoor toilets.

Everyone seemed restless and ready for the program to end so the teacher's treat could be distributed. There was a rustle of relief when Mrs. Nolen announced that an original work by Maureen McCracken would be the last number on the program.

Maureen was so hurried and nervous that she didn't try to slide the safety pins across the wire to close the curtain and set her stage. She tripped over a pile of coats as she went through the cloakroom. At the school door, she almost ran into Skeets leading Yvonne.

She could hardly believe her eyes. The slack rope tied to the porch had an unbuckled collar at the end. Tisket was gone. "Skeets, did you see Tisket? Did you?"

"When I came out to take Yvonne to the toilet, Tisket

was whining and jumping around. I felt sorry for her and turned her loose."

"Turned her loose! She's supposed to be in my play right now."

Skeets gasped. "I didn't know that."

In the distance beyond the playground, they heard Tisket's eager bark. "Here, Tisket, here," Maureen called, but she knew she was wasting her voice. Ordinarily Tisket was obedient, but she could never be called off a rabbit trail. She had whined to be set loose because she'd smelled rabbit.

"You've ruined my Christmas play, Skeets. I hope you're satisfied." Maureen felt like shaking Skeets. "Everybody clapped for you. They'll be laughing at me. Mit and Hazel and all of them."

"I didn't mean to. I'll go tell Mrs. Nolen. She can say there's been a change, and the program is over." When Skeets opened the cloakroom door, Maureen saw Walter sitting at the front desk, still wearing his elf cap.

She held Skeets back. "Wait a second." She whistled, got Walter's attention, and beckoned frantically. As soon as he came to the cloakroom, she slammed the door and snatched off his elf cap. "Walter, Skeets turned Tisket loose. She's off chasing a rabbit. You've got to be Wolverette."

"I won't do it."

"Yes, you will, Walter."

"What will I say?"

"You don't have to say one thing. I'll do the talking."

Walter nodded toward the schoolroom. "How will they know in there I'm a dog?"

"Just hunker down on all fours and act kinda doggy," Maureen said.

"I can't be a dog when I'm a boy."

"You can too," Maureen insisted. "You were an elf, and a dog's more real than an elf."

Skeets picked up Maureen's paper bag of costumes and dumped everything on the floor. "I could make a dog's head out of this bag. I'll take Yvonne to Vido and get a black crayon and scissors from my desk." From the cloakroom door, Maureen watched Skeets trying to get through to her desk. Older boys were pushing and shoving. If Skeets didn't hurry, the last number on the program would be a wrestling match.

Once she came with her crayon, Skeets quickly drew ears, eyes, nose, whiskers, mouth, and tongue on the bag. It was a dog's head all right. She snipped out eye openings and put the bag over Walter's head. "Can you see?"

When Walter nodded, his head rattled. "I'm not supposed to say anything." His voice was muffled.

"All right, we're starting, Walter. When I put this little red coat on you, twist around and try to act grateful." Maureen cleared her throat so she could speak good and loud. She opened the door, and Walter followed her to face the audience.

As Gretchen, the family sock knitter and general drudge, she and her dog Wolverette were applauded. Everyone laughed and enjoyed deep-voiced Hans, hungry Fritz, and the demanding stepmother. The apple-trimmed tree of Act Two was a real surprise, and the final curtain brought stamps and cheers.

Maureen peeked out from behind the curtain. "Hear that, Walter? Folks liked it. You were better than Tisket. A lot more dependable."

Everybody crowded around to compliment Maureen and Walter. Mrs. Nolen said it was the grand finale of the program.

Maureen was gathering up her costumes when Mit reached her. "Maureen, your homemade play was really good." He didn't seem to mind that she had used his clothes without his permission. "I guess you showed everybody what a McCracken could do."

"Did Hazel like it?"

"Said so, said I had a real smart kid sister."

When everything was over and people came out into the gray late afternoon, they had to step over Tisket resting on the porch. Maureen didn't bother to scold her. She felt so good that she opened her bag of candy and gave her a piece of Mrs. Nolen's treat.

On the way home, Walter let Uncle Millard's kids take turns wearing his dog head. There wasn't much left of it by the time the McCrackens came to their lane.

Maureen and Walter went to the barn lot to give Patsy the apples from their play as her Christmas treat. Walter held an apple in the palm of his hand. "Old Patsy's not dead yet."

"Not near, Walter. I think she looks better since Mit has been babying her so much."

Mama had already lit the kitchen lamp. There was no

sunset, and a few snowflakes drifted down. Walter began to whistle what sounded like "Hark, the Herald Angels Sing."

"Walter, that was a close one." Maureen hopped about joyfully. "Instead of herald angels, I almost heard the green-eyed monster roar at Christmas. I've got to hurry now and make some catalogue beads for Skeets."

16.

On Christmas Day, they were only going from McCrackens' to the Wiley place, no more than two miles on the back road, but to Maureen the journey was splendid. Mit drove Patsy hitched to the wagon, and Grandma sat beside him on the wagon seat. She had come to Dotzero on the morning train and hadn't expected to be met with a rig.

The back of the wagon was packed with baskets of squash pies, roast chicken, loaves of homemade bread, jars of green beans, prints of butter, buckets of milk, and a crock of head cheese. Maureen and Walter sat with their legs dangling over the open endgate of the wagon, ready to slide out and walk when Patsy had to pull uphill. Every so often, Grandma turned around and peered between the brim of her hat and the worn fur collar of her coat to see

147

if they were still aboard. Mama and Dad were walking across the fields so there wouldn't be so much strain on Patsy.

As near as Maureen could tell, Walter was trying to whistle "Jingle Bells." She considered a one-horse open wagon at least 100 percent improvement over a one-horse open sleigh. It held more people and required no snow.

They rolled along the narrow road through McCrackens' woods. Wind tore at the last of the russet leaves on the oaks. From the shelter of cedar trees, red cardinals flew across the road. Alder shrubs glowing with red berries stood out among the bare trees.

Against her neck Maureen felt the softness of the gift she'd found that morning under the Christmas tree. Occasionally she unbuttoned her coat to see the beautiful dark red and gold of her silk scarf. It was patterned with odd fruits, gourds and squash cut open to show more designs inside. She'd never seen anything like it and was glad Mama had bought it in Beaumont instead of the wool scarf she needed.

Maureen had expected Mit to give her the Kewpie doll at Christmas, but it wasn't under the Christmas tree for her or for Mama either. While Mit had been hitching up Patsy, Maureen had looked in the bottom drawer of his dresser. The Kewpie was still there. He hadn't given it to Hazel, either.

At the edge of McCrackens' woods, Mit gave Patsy a breather. On one side of the road, the timber went on and on up the steep hill and far ridges of Dotzero State Forest.

148

On the other side, the grass of the Wiley pasture was bleached and dried to the color of corn shucks. A Jersey cow like Molly would not have shown up at all, but Mrs. Wiley's herd of white-faced, red Herefords did. They clustered around the low-roofed feeding barn Uncle Millard had repaired and pulled hay through the bars of the mangers he had filled.

Epitome munched hay with the herd. Maureen hadn't forgotten Mrs. Wiley's promise of a reward for his rescue. Christmas Day was a very likely time for her to present a suitable gift.

Maureen ran ahead to open the gate to the lane that led through the pasture to the Wiley house. Thick, white woodsmoke blowing from the chimney meant a good fire in the sitting room. Only a wisp drifted from the tin flue above the kitchen, so there wasn't much fire in the cookstove. Mama had been right to offer to bring dinner along when she accepted Aunt Cora's invitation for Christmas.

Inside, the kitchen linoleum was dim with dirt, but no one expected it to be clean, even at Christmas, with kids tracking in mud that thawed at midday. She couldn't see much wallpaper, for the tree in the sitting room was big enough for a church. The hand-painted picture was somewhere behind the cedar branches. The tree was decorated with tinfoil ornaments and with bells, Santas, and angels that Skeets had drawn and colored. There wasn't a store-bought ornament on the tree.

Mrs. Wiley had been invited because all her kinfolks were in the Wiley cemetery. She had declined the invitation to dinner, saying she couldn't stand the noise and confusion but would come to see about her cattle that needed attention Christmas Day, same as any other day.

After dinner, Aunt Cora said they should leave the dishes and listen to the end of the Christmas story Uncle Millard had been reading aloud from a Wiley book. Maureen sat on the floor near a window so she could watch for Mrs. Wiley as she listened.

A Christmas Carol, which Uncle Millard read in a good loud voice so he could hear himself, was better than any story in Maureen's reader. With all those ghosts, it made Maureen think of Halloween and Christmas put together. When Uncle Millard had finished, Mama asked to borrow the book so the McCrackens could read the whole story.

Dishwashers were being assigned when Maureen saw Mrs. Wiley's Durant turn in at the lane and stop at the feeding barn. The time seemed good to get out of the crowded house and go wish Mrs. Wiley a merry Christmas. Uncle Millard saw her too and said he'd better see if his boss lady had any instructions for him. In the end, most of the children went along.

Maureen was careful not to be rambunctious around the cattle and spoke in a low voice to Mrs. Wiley. "I think Epitome looks more purebred than ever, don't you?"

She nodded. "He's coming along."

"It was a good thing I heard him bellowing that day he ruined my special apple tree. I'm the one cut the barbed wire and got him out of the fence," Maureen reminded her.

"Oh, I know, Maureen." Mrs. Wiley looked sharply at

her. "I'm not one to forget things done or things left undone. However, there is still something that remains to be seen."

Maureen wondered what it could be. One thing was plain. With so many kids running around, Mrs. Wiley couldn't single Maureen out for a present on Christmas Day. She'd have to give something appropriate to all the children, and Mrs. Wiley wasn't about to do that. She'd already given Uncle Millard's family a house to live in. Even Mr. Scrooge, scared by ghosts, wouldn't do more.

McCrackens left early enough for Patsy to have plenty of time to get them home for chores before dark. The wind had died down, and the sun broke through the clouds to glow like a woods fire through the black tree trunks in the west. Maureen and Walter watched it until it burned away, leaving a sky gray as ash.

"Christmas is over," Walter said.

"It most certainly is not. Not 100 percent over," Maureen contended. "After Patsy has a couple of days to rest, we're going to ride her over to Sansoucies'. I'll make Mama let us."

Two days later, when Maureen asked permission to go, Mama couldn't think of any reason not to give it. Patsy was gentle and didn't stumble at a slow pace. Even so, a horse was a very big animal, and Maureen was a little afraid of riding horseback the day they started for Sansoucies'. She didn't intend to tell anyone, certainly not Walter, who rode behind her holding to the back of the saddle. His short legs stuck out without the support of stirrups that she had. Gradually she got used to being above Patsy's nodding head as she plodded along the wagon trace toward Cold Spring.

"We won't have time to play if you don't make her go faster," Walter said. "Reach up and shake a limb so she'll think you broke off a switch."

They had learned that this trick made her walk faster. Maureen rustled dry oak leaves on an overhanging branch, and Patsy stepped more lively.

She was slow again as they rode by Cold Spring school, and she poked by the big farm with three barns and two silos. Maureen could do nothing to make her speed up when they came within view of the tenant house in which their friends lived.

The outline of the house was blurred by the bare branches of a trumpet creeper clinging to its walls and roof. Low and brown, the house looked as if it might have grown out of the ground along with the vine, whose dry seedpods rattled against the windows.

All the Sansoucies ran out to meet them. "You've come on horseback!" Rose exclaimed, as Maureen tossed her the reins. "What a surprise!"

"No surprise to me," Mrs. Sansoucie said. "This morning I dropped the dish towel twice. That's a sure sign of company."

"You get off and on the left side." Maureen dismounted to demonstrate. "That's one thing you have to remember about a horse. Here, Walter, slide down this side."

Rose tied Patsy to a heavy branch of trumpet vine, and Mrs. Sansoucie urged Maureen to come inside.

"I will directly, but I want to play all the games we used to play together."

Wolf-over-the-ridge, prison base, lemonade—Maureen ran and shouted in the games. Then she slowed down to show the Sansoucies how to play hopscotch.

When they went inside, Maureen and Walter presented her original Christmas play. Even without props, the Sansoucies appreciated it.

"Maybe next time I come, I'll bring my cousin Skeets. She'll put on a regular circus for you," Maureen said. "Now before we go, all of you kids get a turn riding Patsy while Walter leads her. I want to talk to Rose."

Maureen and Rose had a lot to talk about as they walked toward the big farmhouse. Rose pointed out the poles and wires that carried electricity to both the house and barn. Maureen had heard of the Rural Electrification Administration on the radio. She hoped the power lines might eventually reach the McCracken place. Rose told her that sometimes she earned a quarter working for the farmer's wife in the big house.

"Mit had work in the fall. Kinda odd pay. I won't have a chance to make a red cent until summer. Then maybe I'll get paid by the hundred for swatting flies," Maureen said. "Still everybody says I helped sell our pigs and helped Aunt Cora get her new tooth."

"I'd be proud if I'd done all the things you've told me about. Made apple grafts and everything."

"They'll grow, too, into big trees, loaded with wonderful apples, just from a little cambium layer. Dessie and

Skeets would think I was nuts if I tried to tell them about that."

"How are you getting along now with your kinfolks?"

Maureen fingered her silk scarf. "We're getting along, but it's hard as Patsy pulling a full wagon uphill. I showed Dessie my scarf." Maureen imitated a high, whining voice. "Too bad you don't have a place to wear it. Dessie's not so sour about school, though. She sees Melvin Stackhouse working there, and she's struck on him. I think Mit is struck on Hazel Stackhouse, even if he won't own up to it. He doesn't talk to her much, but he's always looking at her when he thinks she's not looking. And he's awful particular about his clothes. He won a Kewpie doll at the fair and didn't give it to anybody, so I think he wants to give it to Hazel as soon as he gets the nerve. At school, Skeets is Mrs. Nolen's pet. I just can't trust Uncle Millard's kids the way I do you. They're waiting to come out with something smart."

"You should have trusted them about that picture show palace. You said you saw it with your own eyes," Rose reminded her.

"Yes, but mostly I can't make them believe anything wonderful ever happens in Dotzero. I wish I could." Maureen smoothed her scarf. "I wish something else, too. I wish I could draw. Make pictures like the one in the Wiley house."

"I guess you could learn. Have somebody teach you," Rose suggested.

Maureen shook her head. "No, you've got to be born able to draw, like being double-jointed." Maureen stopped and looked back. "We've gone far enough. The kids will have Patsy so worn out she won't be able to get Walter and me home."

Rose hurried along with Maureen. "It was a Christmas present to all of us for you and Walter to come visit and put on your play."

Patsy was like a different horse on the way home. She walked faster with no urging. Near the McCracken barn, she broke into a jolting gait, close to a trot.

Mama saw them coming and came to help them un-saddle. "It was all I could do to hold her." Maureen tried not to sound frightened. "She mighty near knocked me and Walter off going right into the barn."

"She wanted to get home. It's going to snow; I can smell it," Mama said. Maureen took a deep breath. There was a sweet sharpness in the air.

At dusk, big flakes began to fall. By bedtime, Maureen could see nothing from her rattling window but slanting, wind-driven snow.

At daylight, the world was white. Maureen grabbed her clothes and went down to dress by the kitchen stove and to listen to the radio weather report of a record snowfall.

Wind and snow kept up all day. Mama wouldn't let Maureen and Walter out of the house except to bring in firewood. That evening the wind stilled, snow finally stopped, and a full moon shone.

Maureen looked at the drift piled below the kitchen window and called Walter to see the sparkling snow. "Now, Walter, you can see for yourself how the moon shines on certain snowflakes. How big is a snowflake?"

Walter touched his thumbnail. "About that big."

"And how many snowflakes fell?"

"Ten billion," Walter said without hesitation.

"And how many miles away is the moon?"

Walter looked up at the silver moon in the cold, clear sky. "Thousands and thousands and thousands."

"Yes, approximately, so what percent chance does one particular little snowflake in our yard have of reflecting the moon?"

"I don't know," Walter admitted.

"Well, I'll tell you. Decimal point-zero-zero-zero-and four more zeros-two percent."

"Approximately?"

"Yes, and don't you forget it, Walter, because you never know—"

Maureen stopped as Mit came into the kitchen.

"I'd forget Maureen's blathering if I were you, Walter." Mit took the sixteen-gauge shotgun from the rack over the door and got the gun cleaner from the chimney shelf. "I'm going to put meat on the table. Going hunting the first thing in the morning." Tisket pricked up her ears, left her warm spot by the stove, and whined eagerly. "Go back to sleep, Tisket. You can't go. I'd lose you in the snow drifts. I won't need a dog to track rabbits tomorrow."

Mit was right. Maureen and Walter saw rabbit tracks everywhere when they went out the next morning.

"The storm has abated, so let's abound," Maureen shouted, as she floundered through difts. "Let's see if my grafts got through the storm."

Four tops and a bit of their trunks showed above the

drift. The protective wire cylinders around the trunks were deep under the snow. As she came closer to the trees, Maureen was dismayed to see the snow around them patterned with rabbit tracks. A band of raw wood girdled two trees. Rabbits had hopped on the deep snow above the wire protectors and eaten through the bark and cambium layer all around the trunks.

Maureen ran her gloved finger around the grooves in the trunks. "These two are goners for sure, Walter. Girdled trees die. But the others look all right. Help me dig down to the rabbit guards, so these two won't be eaten too."

Walter started to dig. "There's still a smidgin."

"And we've lost half of it. Fifty percent of our smidgen." Maureen uncovered a guard and pulled snow away from it.

17

The first snow of the winter was the deepest. Afterward only a few inches fell. The ground was bare by February, but there was no warmth in the sun.

Dad was huddled by the cookstove fire when Maureen and Walter came in from school. He sure was out of heart. Maureen thought of something interesting that might cheer him up. "I just can't get over 33 and ⅓ percent. Three, that's an odd number. But if you add up thirty-three and a third three times, that whole mess of threes, you get a nice round one hundred."

"Thirty-three and a third percent, 'one-third of the nation ill-housed, ill-clad, ill-nourished.' That's how Roosevelt put it." Dad's voice was dismal, and he didn't look up at Maureen. She was glad when Mama returned from Uncle Millard's.

Mama's cheeks were pink from the cold, and her eyes sparkled. "When the days begin to lengthen and the cold begins to strengthen. That's what they say about February. It's true all right. We can do chores by daylight."

"How is it over there?" Dad nodded toward the Wiley place.

"Enough flour, meal, lard, and potatoes, wood to keep warm, but not enough shoe leather for the kids to walk to school in this cold. They are all home, and Oren has them scared half to death reading stories of Edgar Allan Poe from a Wiley book. Millard wonders if the hay for Mrs. Wiley's herd will last until grass starts."

"We won't have to guess about that here this spring," Dad said gloomily. "We'll have to put out cash for more hay and corn to keep Molly and that old horse and the chickens alive."

Maureen leaned against Dad's shoulder. "February is my favorite month, absolute favorite," she announced. "Everything is ahead—spring—and school won't last forever. This year my apple grafts might bloom. Then there will be summer and good things to eat from the garden and swimming. Everything's ahead."

"Too far ahead," Dad said. "The Hunger Moon. That's what the Indians called February."

"Oh, now, Cleve, we'll manage." Mama tried to sound cheerful. "Spring will come. Work on the extra gang will start up."

"Spring! Johnson grass will start up, take over the bottom field. Sprouts will spead in the ridge field, brambles in the meadow. We can't put in crops. Next February will be worse. All I can do is let more go." Dad got up, put on his mackinaw, and went out into the cold.

"I didn't have any luck trying to cheer him up, either," Maureen said.

Mama put her arms around Maureen and Walter. "He had to decide something that was hard for him."

"What, Mama?" Maureen asked.

"He'll tell you sometime, but don't ask him about it now, Maureen. Just leave him alone."

That evening Maureen tried not to bother anyone. After Walter went to bed, she sat on the edge of the sitting-room carpet and played jacks on the bordering bare floor. Jacks was a town game; Skeets was good at it. By spring, Maureen intended to be as good, maybe even better, than Skeets. It wasn't her fault that Mit stepped on a stray jack in his sock feet and yelled that his foot was broken.

Then all was quiet except for the plunk of the little rubber ball and the rattle of the tossed jacks on the bare floor. A *hoot-hoot* echoed from McCrackens' woods.

Walter came downstairs, crying. "There it is again. I heard it."

Mama put down the Wiley book she was reading. "Walter, I thought you were sound asleep. What's the matter?"

"The mystery of the mountains. Maureen told me." The *hoot-hoot* call came nearer. Walter buried his head in Mama's lap.

"Oh, I like to hear the hoot owls, Walter. It's a good sign," Mama assured him. "They start calling this time of year because they know winter is over. Time to get nest-

160

ing. Maureen, he's finally got over the freak tent, and now you've got him on something else. Mystery of the mountains, my foot."

"I was telling him the truth," Maureen defended herself. "You take this big hoot owl. How does he know it's near spring when it's still cold as kraut? He hasn't got any calendar or newspaper or almanac or anything. That's what I call mystery. Of course, he might of heard a radio news report and—"

"That's enough, Maureen," Dad said. "Go back upstairs with him."

Maureen took the flashlight and shone it in the corners of the hall and up the stairway. She always looked for robbers and burglars. Sometimes she wondered what the difference was between the two.

Walter crawled into his bed, but he didn't want Maureen to go downstairs. "Stay until I get sleepy."

"It's too cold standing here." Maureen shivered. "I want to practice jacks so I can beat Skeets."

"What do you think Dad had to decide that made him worried?" Walter asked.

"Couldn't say, Walter."

"Do you think Mit knows?"

Maureen hugged herself against the cold. "Maybe. Sometimes they tell him things because he's older. But he's too bigheaded to tell us. So don't ask him. Go to sleep now."

"I'm not sleepy," Walter insisted. "Tell me about Johnson grass."

"I've told you so often you could tell me." Still, it was

nice to have a listener. Maureen wrapped up in a quilt from Mit's bed.

"There was this man, Mr. J. G. Johnson, John Greenleaf Johnson," Maureen began. "He was boss of the biggest railroad in the United States. Everything on his railroad was running right on the dot the way a railroad is supposed to, and towns were getting bigger and bigger, turning into regular cities, all along his railroad. And people were going everywhere and shipping everything. And Mr. Johnson was getting richer and richer. Everything was fine except for one thing. Every time it rained hard in the Saint Francois Mountains, and it mostly rained hard there, *ker-wham*, out washed a big hunk of railroad bank and in caved the whole track. All the trains stopped. Nobody could go anywhere or get anything. People were mad, and Mr. J. G. Johnson was about to get laid off his own railroad. He had to put a stop to it, so he went to China.

"And while he was there looking at houses with turned-up roofs and this big wall and everything, he saw a plant growing all over the side of a steep mountain. There wasn't any gulley or washout on that mountain. 'What's that stuff?' he asked, and the Chinese folks said something he couldn't understand.

"He tried to pull some up. Couldn't. So the Chinese folks helped pull and tug and finally hauled up a big white root, bigger than a sweet potato.

"Then just like a light bulb coming on in the funny paper, Mr. Johnson got this bright idea. 'I'm taking this root home in my suitcase to plant on my railroad banks. And then no matter how hard it rains, my railroad banks

162

won't wash out, my tracks won't cave in, and my trains won't stop running.'

"And that's what he did. He named it Johnson grass after himself. He thought that was better than his name on a tombstone after he died. First thing you know, Johnson grass was growing on railroad banks in Missouri, Arkansas, Tennessee." Maureen jumped up and pointed in all directions. "Kentucky, Alabama, Mississippi, California . . . just about everywhere. And those roots held the banks and there were no more washouts, no more track cave-ins, no more late trains. And that's the end."

" 'Tis not."

"Could be, for a happy ending, but that was just the start of that greedy grass. Railroads go on level ground, like Lost Creek bottomland. You know that. So Johnson grass roots just crept under the right-of-way fences into the rich bottom fields and choked out the corn.

"The farmers plowed it out with mules and hacked it out with hoes and had their wives and children and their kinfolks pull it out, but they couldn't get rid of it. Johnson grass is harder to fight than a flock of fleas, and J. G. Johnson would have done better to have put his name on a tombstone."

Walter was so quiet that Maureen flashed her light to see if he had fallen asleep. Walter sat up in bed. "I told Mit that story. He says it's a pack of lies. He says Farmer Johnson planted the grass for hay, and the seeds blew around."

Maureen sat on the edge of Walter's bed. "Mit! what does he know? He doesn't even know how to start to talk to a nice girl like Hazel, who likes him. He doesn't know what's going to happen next, does he?"

"No, what is?" Walter asked.

"It's not easy to say for sure." Maureen thought for a few moments. "Near as I can make out, some kind of spooky thing is going to come out of the ground . . . and . . . it will be the Ghost of Summer Past," she said brightly. "It will move over our bottom field in the fog of the night, flow around, and *whammo,* no more Johnson grass. Next day it will all be gone and the ground dried out and mellow, ready for Patsy to plow."

"Will that spooky thing get rid of Old Whisker out of our swimming hole?" Walter asked.

"Nope, it can't work on land and water both. You'll have to get in there just the same, kick your feet, and paddle your hands."

"Skeets says there is no water monster in Lost Creek," Walter reported.

"Walter, we know more about Lost Creek than she does," Maureen reminded him. "Once that old monster bumped into Mit with his whisker. It felt like a baseball bat. Of course, if he is just a nice granddaddy catfish, somebody might catch him this spring. He might not be much bigger than you are."

"Hoo-hoo, hoo," came a cry from the dark .

"Are you sure that's an owl, Maureen?"

"It sounds a little different," she whispered.

"There's a ghost down in the ground beside Lost Creek and a monster in the water." Walter pulled the quilts over his head.

164

Maureen shone her flashlight at the cold blackness of the window. A single yellow eye stared back at her. Unknowns had joined possible robbers and burglars in the hall. Even with the flashlight, she couldn't go out there.

"Mit! Mit!" she called, "aren't you ever coming upstairs? It's way past your bedtime."

18

By daylight, Lost Creek and the bottom field weren't frightening at all, but to Maureen they were still extraordinary. Ice lingered as a lacy white trim at the edge of the water. The deep swimming hole reflecting the gray March sky held mystery. Unchanged by winter, the bottom field seemed to be waiting for something. Long stems of coarse Johnson grass lay as if combed in place by the last high water over the rich ground.

Winter's thaw brought all Uncle Millard's kids back to school. One evening, coming home, Skeets raced ahead across the bridge with her yellow hair flying and tangling in the raveling yarn of her knit cap.

"I don't see why you always stop on this bridge," Dessie said to Maureen. "There's nothing to see but water and dirt." She walked on.

166

"Come on, Walter, I'll show you how to skip stones." Maureen and Walter ran from the bridge and jumped down to the gravel bar at the edge of the water. She selected a small, flat stone and showed him how to hold it horizontally to the water. She drew her arm far back and flung the stone, which skipped twice before it sank.

Another stone fluttered along the top of the water like a swallow after gnats. Without looking around, she knew Skeets had skipped it. Maureen dropped her second stone and said she and Walter had to get home at once and help Dad. She could see him working on the north orchard slope.

Maureen didn't bother to change from her school clothes or see that Walter did either before they started for the orchard where thin wisps of smoke rose. The three big heaps of orchard prunings that had been near the fence for a year were now three wide circles of glowing embers.

Dad always burned the previous year's piles of dry prunings in March. He called that job "getting the jump on spring." Under the fires, all the pesty weed seeds were killed as the ground was warmed for early planting of fescue and red-top grasses.

Nearby Dad was pruning a big Baldwin apple tree. "Can I help sow grass seed again this spring?" Maureen asked. "The seed I planted last year came up thick as hair on a dog's back."

"I'll need all the help I can get," Dad said. "I want to finish the home jobs. There's no wind today, so I got the jump on spring burning brush. Good weather's coming, and any day now I might get called to work on the extra gang."

Dad wasn't whistling a tune, but the prospect of paid work put him in a good humor. He had pruned a heap from the apple tree, and he was still lopping off limbs.

"Are you sure you're not overdoing it?" Maureen asked.

Dad stood back and looked at the tree. "They say if you don't have more limbs on the ground than you leave on the tree, you haven't pruned enough. The sun shines into a thinned tree to color the apples." A fat robin flew to a perch in the pruned tree. "All kinds of spring signs. Millard came to tell us about new calves at the Wiley place. Mama and Mit went galavantin' over there to see them."

"Last night I heard peeper frogs. They sounded better to me than a mockingbird singing," Maureen said.

Dad stopped pruning to watch a car coming up from Lost Creek. Usually Maureen knew every car that appeared in the lane, but she didn't recognize this blue Model A Ford.

"Who's that?" she asked.

Dad studied the car for a moment. "A fellow I've got to do some business with." Dad leaned his long-handled pruners against the tree.

"We're going too," Maureen said.

"No. I have to take care of this. You stay and start a new brush pile."

They followed Dad to the orchard gate and watched him get in the car and drive away toward McCrackens' woods.

168

"Who is it, Maureen?"

"Walter, you expect me to know everything." Maureen turned to inspect her two grafted trees planted near the gate. "See how straight this little tree stood all winter? It's well rooted, I can tell." She ran her finger along a twig. "It's got leaf buds, and it won't be long until they'll show green. It might even have a flower bud."

Walter started to pinch off the bug-sized brown bump on the twig. Maureen held his hand. "Not off this tree. It can't spare a single bud. Over there at that Grimes Golden, I'll show you how you can tell if a fruit bud made it through the winter and didn't get nipped by late freeze."

Maureen broke open a bud with her thumbnail to show the tiny, packed pale stamens of an apple blossom. "It's alive all right. If it had been killed, there would be nothing but a little black dot."

"Could you make a tree bud the way a person makes a radio?" Walter asked.

"I guess you could, but it would never grow into an apple blossom," she said, as she stooped to gather scattered prunings.

When she straightened up, a breeze soft as milkweed down brushed her cheek. Then a sudden gust blew up from Lost Creek. She heard crackling and turned to see that the circles of smoldering coals had burst into flames. The wind blew sparks into the dry leaves and grass. Tongues of fire spread. The wind rose fast as fear.

Walter stamped at the flames. "Not in your school

169

shoes!" Maureen yelled. "Here, use this." She tore a piece from a rotted burlap bag she had found on the ground.

While they beat out fire in one place, it started in another nearer the barn. Soon their burlap pieces were smoldering.

"Run! Ring the bell. Ring it hard," Maureen gasped. "Get shovels, packing shed."

In eye-stinging smoke she fell over a rake. With all her strength, she used it to beat out flames licking toward the barn. The farm bell rang and rang. The sound echoed from the state forest hill, but nobody came. Where could all her family and kinfolks be? Maureen had never felt so alone.

Suddenly, through thick, choking smoke, Mit appeared and took her rake. "Go pump water," he shouted.

Then Maureen saw Mama fighting fire. For a terrible moment, she thought Mama's blowing apron was blazing. "Where's Walter? Where is he?" Maureen screamed.

Mama beat at flames with a shovel. "At the well. Get buckets and help him pump."

As Maureen ran toward the well, she saw Aunt Cora, Oren, Vido, and Dessie racing to the orchard with sacks and rakes. The Model A Ford careened back from McCrackens' woods. The stranger driving the car slammed on the brakes. Dad and Uncle Millard jumped out and outran him to the fire.

Maureen and Walter filled big buckets, little pails, pots, pans, anything that would hold water. Skeets, Buddy, Boots, even Mertie carried water for Mit to throw

170

on the side of the barn that steamed with heat. Chigger and Yvonne stayed out from underfoot.

A pickup truck driven too fast for conditions on the back road rounded the turn into the McCracken place. Two men as dressed up as if they were going to church got out and strapped tanks to their backs. From the Missouri state emblem on the door, Maureen knew it was a Dotzero State Forest truck. She and Walter had no more vessels to fill. Maureen was so exhausted that she could hardly force her legs to take her back to the orchard.

There the foresters put out the last of the fire with the chemicals from their tanks.

Dad leaned against a charred fence post and tried to get his breath. "Now that was a dang fool thing . . . for me . . . to do," he panted. His face and hands were black smudged, his eyes red rimmed. He didn't look like himself with his eyebrows singed away. Maureen felt her own eyebrows. They were coarse and curly from the heat of fire.

"I went off and left these kids with coals smoking." Dad put a heavy hand on Maureen's shoulder. She couldn't tell if it was for support or to tell her he was relieved she hadn't been burned. "It had been still as death all day long, and I'd raked dry stuff well away before I set the fires. Never dreamed the wind would rise like that."

"This was more excitement than I bargained for," the stranger said. He went to his car and drove away.

The men from the state forest were in no hurry to leave. They wanted to make sure the fire was completely out. "For a while there, we thought you had a bad one going," one of the men said. "Of course, we were in the fire tower. This fire season before spring green-up is worse than fall fire season. We saw your bonfires, but without any wind they didn't seem to threaten state lands."

"Millard, Cora, Oren, Skeets—all of you—it's a blessing you folks were here to help," Dad said.

Aunt Cora tucked stray locks of her red hair into the loose twist on top of her head. She looked around and accounted for all her children. "I'm careful of fire. It's like the Scripture says: 'And there rose up fire out of the rock.'"

"This one didn't rise out of a rock. I miscalculated." Dad shook his head.

Mama had Walter by the hand. "We could have had a burnout, lost the orchard, the barn, and everything if Maureen and Walter hadn't spread the alarm. Soon as I heard that bell I took off running."

"As it is, I don't think you're hurt too much." The forester walked over blackened ground to the Grimes Golden apple tree. "Some damage here, but a big tree like this will probably live." He glanced toward the gate. "The young trees are killed."

For a second, Maureen didn't realize that the two bare sticks, burned black as the surrounding ground, were her grafts. She began to cry. "How could they burn when they were green wood, alive just a little while ago?" she sobbed.

"Anything will burn if it gets hot enough," the forester said, as if Maureen's grafts from the wonderful wild apple tree were nothing special.

"It's a shame about these little grafts." Dad broke off one of the black sticks. "But you sure helped save some of our best bearing trees. You know how to graft. We'll make more."

"Can't be any more like that." Maureen tried to keep from crying in front of everybody, but her nose ran from sniffling. When she wiped it with her hand, she left a black smear across her face and her singed eyebrows.

"You look awful," Mit said.

"I don't care," she snapped at him. "I don't care 'bout this old place or anything!"

"Well, don't get so huffy," Mit said. "I think you showed a lot of gumption fighting the fire and ringing for help. Everybody thinks so, but you still look awful."

"Leave me alone, Mit McCracken," she shrieked.

They all stood around visiting as if nothing terrible had happened.

Walter followed Maureen through the orchard gate. "Is that the last smidgen?"

"You know it is." Maureen no longer tried not to cry.

19

A few weeks later Maureen stood on the bridge and looked at the creek and the bottom field. Dessie was right. They were just water and dirt. If she had let herself, she would have felt as shriveled and black as a frosted apple-blossom bud, but she looked above the part of the orchard still black from the fire to McCrackens' woods. There leaf buds swelled in a tide of pink, cream, and peach. The far ridge of the state forest was lavender and rose. "Green-up time," the foresters called it, but green leaves were still to come.

Along the shortcut path, maple trees bloomed with tiny crimson flowers and baby leaves almost as red as their fall foliage had been. Hickory buds opened like pale hands unclasping. Maureen marveled at all the pastel colors of spring and tried to forget the buds that wouldn't open on her grafted trees.

The pasture was bright green with grass for Molly and Patsy. Still Dad stayed in a wintry mood, waiting for a call to work. Maureen knew how he felt, but she didn't try to talk him out of his bleak mood.

Mama's pink sassafras tea that was supposed to thin sluggish winter blood didn't perk Maureen up. She came home from school alone and complained to Mama. "Walter is turning into a regular smart aleck. I told him to come on home, but he just sassed me and went with Skeets. They're going to fly kites in the Wiley pasture."

Mama looked up at the clear, windswept sky. "I can't say that I blame him. Why don't you change your clothes and go too?"

"I don't want to."

"What's wrong, Maureen?" Mama brushed back wisps of hair that had blown into Maureen's eyes. "You act like life has a pick on you."

"You should see what crummy kites Skeets makes," Maureen grumbled. "The sticks are heavy as kindling, and she tears up all Aunt Cora's good rags for kite tails."

Soon afterward, however, kites bobbed over the Wiley pasture and rose steadily to sail in the blue sky. Maureen could almost feel the tug on the string as the wind took a kite still higher. That tug was as exciting as the pull on a fishline from an unknown catch deep in Lost Creek. Mama hadn't given her an after-school job; she could run over there. But she went only as far as the tire swing,

175

where she sat and wondered why she sometimes couldn't make herself do something she really wanted to do.

School went on and on, come day, go day, hope for Friday. There would be no unexplainable wonder from her own hill farm to show anyone. Instead, her cousins had shown her that movies really were shown in a palace where you could pretend you were a princess for the price of a ticket. Maureen thought of the picture that showed a building made of stone lace and wondered if it too might be real. She borrowed the Wiley book that it was in and took it to school. At recess, she stayed at her desk.

"Inside on a day like this? What ails you, Maureen?" Mrs. Nolen looked up from papers she was grading at her desk. "You're extra quiet these days. Have you got spring fever?"

"My blood might be sluggish, for one thing." Maureen thought of her blood, thick and dark red. She took the Wiley book to Mrs. Nolen's desk. "I don't think I've got anything, though. I feel more like I've lost something, but I don't know what it is." She tried not to loosen the slick-coated page from the binding as she showed Mrs. Nolen the picture of Reims Cathedral. "Is there any such place as this?"

"Of course," Mrs. Nolen said at first glance. "Do you have doubts about it?"

"I never saw anything like it." Maureen turned to another picture. It showed what looked like a mountain rising out of the sea, but it too seemed to be made of stone-lace buildings. "How about this?"

"Mont-Saint-Michel. That's real too." Mrs. Nolen looked up at Maureen. "Being from Missouri, the Show-Me State, maybe you'll have to be shown. You might talk yourself over to France sometime and see for yourself." Mrs. Nolen looked at the name in the front of the book. "You'll see things the Wileys only read about."

Maureen put the book far back in her desk so her cousins wouldn't see it and ask why she'd brought it to school. There was no use reminding them of her past ignorance. She preferred to think of what her teacher had said about her future. Mrs. Nolen seemed to think a person could do most anything. Maureen liked that idea.

That evening, when she and Walter stopped as usual on the bridge, Melvin Stackhouse came along with a heavy bamboo fishing pole over his shoulder. "Been fishing down at the swimming hole all afternoon." He tested his fishline. "Got me a strong one. I'm going to catch that big catfish everybody talks about. I didn't get a bite today, but I'll get him."

"Right now you better get sweeping," Maureen said. "School's been out a long time, and Dessie's waiting for a glimpse of you."

They watched him lurch down the road. "He's going to catch Old Whisker," Maureen scoffed. "He'll do well if he doesn't hook himself in the seat of the pants. He hasn't lived at Dotzero hardly any time, and he's going to catch him. Mit has tried and tried. He would dearly love to catch him to show off to Hazel Stackhouse. Do you know who's going to land him, Walter?"

"Uncle Millard?"

"No, we are. You and I will use a secret bait."

"What if it's a water monster?"

"Then we'll catch us a water monster. That doesn't happen every day, not even in Lost Creek at Dotzero in the Saint Francois Mountains."

As if a monster had heard her words, lightning flashed over the water and thunder rumbled. The sky in the south was dark as a pocket. For good luck, they hopped on each rock step of their shortcut path up the hill and ran across the yard in lashing rain.

It was still pouring when Maureen went to bed, and she liked the sound of the rain on the tin roof. By morning, when the rain slackened, Lost Creek had spread over the low bottomland, but the road up to the bridge was well above the swift water.

Water stood on the fields for several humid days. In sunny hours it flashed silver. Under storm clouds it darkened and rose high from hard showers. There were no crops to ruin, for the fields had not been planted. The water went down gradually, leaving long sloughs of backwater in the bottomland. Debris from the flood matted the fences and overhanging willow branches.

McCrackens' bottom field gave off a stagnant low-water smell. Maureen advised Walter to hold his nose as they went by their land on the way to school. All week she had reported flood changes to Mrs. Nolen. It was Friday before she remembered to go to the store and ask for mail. She thought all her cousins, even Dessie, had already started home and was surprised when Skeets ran ahead of her and Walter into the store.

Mrs. Stackhouse was not at the postal window. "Any mail for McCracken?" Maureen called out.

"Or O'Neil?" Skeets chimed in.

"I'm over here," Mrs. Stackhouse said from behind the dry-goods counter, "and I can see that your pigeonholes are empty. I've been looking for you to come in, Maureen. I understand that your good bottom field is just ruined by this high water."

"Why, it is not any such thing! It has fine flood dirt washed over it. Better than ever," Maureen asserted.

"Melvin was down there fishing. He told us the field is all gouged out, water standing in it. It will be just a worthless piece of land for your folks to pay taxes on. Like as not, they will want to get rid of it now."

"We couldn't do that, Mrs. Stackhouse! It's part of our place. It'll drain out, sweeten up, and we'll put in a crop of corn with old Patsy."

"Patsy!" Mrs. Stackhouse smiled in amusement.

"She's still alive," Walter announced. "Not dead by spring, the way—"

"That's enough, Walter." Maureen nudged him.

Mrs. Stackhouse was so short and wide that she had to lean across the counter to see Skeets's shoes. "My land, honey, what have you got on your feet?"

Skeets stooped and pressed the empty toes of the high-topped shoes. "Oren outgrew these. Dessie won't wear them, so I have to until school's out."

Mrs. Stackhouse straightened boxes of shoes on the shelf. "Your mother will get pay from the sewing room next week. She could come in and get you a fitting pair. You'd better give those big brogans to Maureen. They're a mile too big for you. Can you still run in those things?"

"Sorta," Skeets said.

As if to prove it, Skeets set off in a run as they left the store and soon disappeared down the road.

"If she hadn't kept running on sharp rocks and if she'd changed her shoes after school, she wouldn't have to wear those awful things now." Maureen sighed.

"You wouldn't like to wear shoes like that," Walter said.

"Of course I wouldn't, Walter, and I wish she didn't either. Shoes are troublesome. You can't grow them, and you can't make them. But sometimes you can't do without them. I'll be glad when it's barefoot weather."

They took their time going home. Maureen showed Walter the bloom on a pawpaw bush as proof that a flower could be almost black. The purple wild verbenas they gathered had the sweetest fragrance of all the spring flowers.

Tisket met them at the bridge. Maureen patted her head as she looked down at the sparkling water by a new gravel bar the flood had deposited.

"Skeets is over there in the bottom field." Walter pointed. "What's she doing?"

As they watched, Skeets circled a large pool of backwater. Then she raised a piece of heavy driftwood and

180

struck hard again and again at something that thrashed in the muddy water.

Maureen and Walter shouted, and Tisket barked as they set out across the field. Maureen's feet felt like lead as mud caked her shoes. "What is it, Skeets?" she called.

"Some big thing." Skeets clubbed away but now seemed unable to move from the mud at the edge of the pool.

In the splashing, Maureen caught a glimpse of a slick, black shape. With a sucking sound, Skeets pulled her feet out of her big shoes. Leaning far forward, she grasped the broad head of an enormous fish and pulled it partly out of the water. She slipped on the mud and fell backward. The huge fish flopped and lashed water with its tail. Tisket barked furiously. On her feet again faster than the fish could recover, Skeets got another hold. Maureen helped her pull it clear of the water. The black head was wider than a big frying pan. The whiskers were bigger than buggy whips.

"It's Old Whisker!" Maureen exclaimed. "You caught Old Whisker."

Walter examined the fish. Faint movements of the gills were the only signs of life. "It's a jumbo-size catfish."

"Monstrous big," Maureen said. "You caught it, Skeets."

"I didn't exactly catch it. I think I stunned it with my stick so we could pull it out."

"You landed it! You landed Old Whisker!" Maureen was still excited.

"When I came to the bridge, I thought I'd stop the

way you do and have a good look at things. I wondered what was moving in this pool. So I picked up that stick and whacked it. I didn't know it was so big," Skeets admitted.

"I remember when you were scared of a yellow jacket. Made an awful fuss about one," Maureen reminded her. "Just a little while at Dotzero, and you're brave enough to land Old Whisker."

"Catfish don't sting," Skeets said.

Walter looked at the muddy slough. "How did he get in there?"

"He had a nice home in Lost Creek, even had fun scaring people that came swimming," Maureen said. "Then the flood washed him out and left him stranded in the backwater."

Skeets sat down and pulled off her muddy stockings. "I lost Oren's shoes."

"You can get them when the mud dries." Maureen looked at her own shoes. "I didn't lose mine, but I just about ruined them. You stay here and guard your fish. Don't let Tisket get hold of it. We'll go home for the wheelbarrow."

"It wasn't a monster after all, was it?" Walter tried to hop over the wettest places.

"Not exactly, Walter."

"You said we'd catch it," Walter reminded her.

"By rights the flood caught Old Whisker, Walter, and don't you forget it."

20_

Aunt Cora thought there was just one thing to do with a fish that size. She wanted to have a big fish fry and invite everyone who had helped them through the winter at Dotzero.

Mr. Stackhouse took soda water out of the cooler so there would be room to keep the fish on ice until Sunday. He said he and Mrs. Stackhouse, Melvin and Hazel would sure come. Mrs. Wiley had been at the place looking at her calves the day the fish was landed. Aunt Cora invited her first thing. She was to pass the word to Grandma in Beaumont. Mrs. Nolen said she and her husband would be there with bells on.

"I sure wish Sansoucies could come," Maureen said. "I haven't seen them since Christmas. I don't want to go unless they come."

Mama held her hands far apart as if measuring. "Big as that fish is, it might not be enough for so many. Besides I don't know how you could get word to them. There isn't time to drop them a penny postcard."

"Walter and I can ride Patsy over there and tell them about the fish fry tomorrow. I think I could catch her. She stays way in the upper pasture eating so much good grass she's getting fat. She needs exercise."

Mama shook head. "No, Patsy's got to stay close to home. No question about that. Let's see, we've got enough potatoes for home fries, enough apples for sauce. I'll gather wild greens. We've got lard and butter for frying, but we're low on cornmeal to roll the fish in. So that means a trip to the store, Maureen. While you're there you can try to get in touch with Sansoucies by telephone at Cold Spring. Mrs. Stackhouse will know how to reach the people they work for."

Maureen went without complaining. She didn't like to spend any of Saturday on a trip to the store, but she knew she'd feel better at the fish fry, with everybody bragging about Skeets, if she had her friend Rose around.

"Well, I'm back," she greeted Mrs. Stackhouse. "I'm keeping the road hot between here and home. I helped wheel the big fish down here. Now I'm back for cornmeal."

"We're all looking forward to the fish fry," Mrs. Stackhouse said. "Hazel's making herself a new dress to wear, so I'm getting no help now from that girl." Mrs. Stackhouse put the heavy white paper bag of meal on the counter. "Are you sure this is enough?"

"It's all I can carry. And now I want to make a long distance telephone call to reach Sansoucies at Cold Spring."

Mrs. Stackhouse took out McCrackens' store account pad. "That's fifteen cents. I'll put it on your bill, too."

Maureen followed her to the telephone in the ware-room, where Mrs. Stackhouse stood on a little step to reach the crank and ring the Beaumont operator. The operator took a while to get the right rings on the Cold Spring party line. Finally, someone answered.

Mrs. Stackhouse turned to Maureen. "Now what's the message?"

"I'll talk." Maureen took the receiver and stumbled over the step to get close to the wall telephone.

"Hello! Hello!" she hollered into the mouthpiece. She heard a faint response. Since someone was there, she thought it best to shout out her message and hope it got through.

"Yes, I can hear you," the voice crackled. "If you want to tell Rose yourself, you can. She's here today helping me with spring cleaning."

Rose's voice sounded familiar but shaky. "I can tell that's really you, Rose." Then Maureen invited all the Sansoucies to the fish fry.

"I'll beg and beg my folks to come. Maybe we can."

"You sound scared, Rose."

"I never talked on a telephone before. Listen, Maureen, we were talking about you just today." Rose spoke so loud that Maureen had to move the receiver away from her ear. "Can you hear me?"

Maureen nodded, then spoke. "Clear as a bell, Rose."

"Look for a visitor at your place, a dressed-up fellow. He was here asking about this girl who gave away apples at the Beaumont Fair. I said that sounds like Maureen, and we told him how to get to your place. Can you still hear me?"

"Yes, when's he coming?" Maureen's voice was a little weaker from excitement.

"I don't know. He might have trouble finding Dotzero. He's looked and looked for you. All he remembers is that you told him you lived on Lost Creek."

"We'll watch for him, and, just think, I might see you tomorrow."

Maureen turned and bumped into Mrs. Stackhouse, who was right behind her. "What do you think that fellow wants, Maureen?"

"I know what he wants." Maureen was confident. "He wants to give me Beaumont County Fair first prize for apples. I guess his conscience got to bothering him, just wouldn't let him alone. So he's making a special trip here to our place to give me a prize on that wild apple I found."

"Oh, I don't know, after all this time." Mrs. Stackhouse was doubtful. "And you told us it wasn't rightfully entered."

"It should have been," Maureen insisted. "Anyway, he's headed for Dotzero. I've got to get home to be there when he comes."

"If he shows up here at the store, we'll give him directions to your place," Mrs. Stackhouse promised.

Maureen would not have been surprised if a car had overtaken her on the way home. A dressed-up man would get out, tip his Panama hat to her, apologize for being late, pin a big rosette on her, and give her a cash prize. Of course, if he showed up at suppertime when Mit and Dad were home, that would be better. The best time of all for him to appear would be the next day in the middle of the fish fry when everybody would be on hand to see her get the prize.

At home, Mama was tired from her work of getting ready for the fish fry and was glad to sit down on a kitchen chair and hear Maureen's puzzling news. She was even more doubtful than Mrs. Stackhouse about a late award.

Maureen wanted to go right back to the bridge and wait for the visitor. She was prepared to stay all afternoon if necessary, but Mama needed her to make the applesauce for the next day. Walter was posted there instead to direct any stranger up the McCracken lane.

Maureen looked out the kitchen window with every apple she peeled. Anxiously she listened for the sound of a car. Dad and Mit finished work in the orchard and changed their clothes so they wouldn't smell like rotten eggs from the sulphur spray they had used.

Finally a car drove up the hill. Maureen had just time to take off her apple-stained apron and wash her hands before the visitor was at the back door. He wore a peaked wool cap instead of a Panama hat, but she recognized him even without his judge's badge of purple ribbon. She was glad she'd washed, for he shook her hand as if he were running for office. "Young lady, I've had a time chasing you down. I'm Lyman Kleinschmidt, and now I know you're Maureen McCracken."

Mama steered everybody out of the messy kitchen to the sitting room. Lyman Kleinschmidt leaned back in the rocker that Mama had insisted he take. "I'd have saved myself a heap of trouble if I had written down McCracken and Dotzero when I first socked my teeth into that apple Maureen brought to the fair.

"As it was, I saved one for my boss there at Knocker Nursery. He took one bite and said to me, 'Kleinschmidt, we want this apple. Go back to Beaumont and get it.'

"So back I went and talked to the fair officials. They had no record. One lady remembered Maureen but had no idea where she lived. All I could remember was Lost Creek, and it's a long, meandering stream here in these hills."

"Saint Francois Mountains," Maureen corrected. She was sitting on the edge of a straight chair so she could jump right up to receive whatever was offered.

Mama held her finger to her lips. "Sit back and listen to Mr. Kleinschmidt."

"I gave up my search for the winter and hit the road again this spring while I was delivering nursery stock. I think I've finally come to the right place. Those apples Maureen gave me when I judged the fair were unpropagated, uncultivated, unidentified, weren't they, Mr. McCracken?"

Maureen didn't give Dad a chance to answer. "I could identify them. Best kind ever was."

Mr. Kleinschmidt kept looking at Dad. "And they were from a tree here on your place, your property?"

"I found it. Walter was with me," Maureen stated.

Mit stretched out a long leg to give her a kick. "Shut up, Maureen."

Mr. Kleinschmidt stood up to make an announcement. "Knocker Nursery wants the rights to this tree, to propagate it and market the stock. We want to make you a suitable offer of compensation."

Dad looked stricken. He shook his head.

Everyone was silent. Then Mama nervously cleared her throat. "We'd like that too. We could do with suitable compensation, but we've had some bad luck with that tree."

Maureen pointed out the window. "It's grassing over now up in the orchard where the grafts burned. Epitome, that's Mrs. Wiley's bull, broke the main tree all to pieces. I made four grafts. Rabbits ate two. The other two lived all winter. Burned up in the spring." Maureen could hardly finish. "So that apple is gone, every smidgen."

Mr. Kleinschmidt picked up his cap and turned it in his hands. "It was a long shot. It's only about once in a couple of generations that a chance wild apple is that good. A long shot, and I guess we all missed."

As they walked toward the gate, Dad talked with Mr. Kleinschmidt. All the McCrackens followed him to his car. Even in his disappointment, Dad remembered his manners. "It's a long way home for you. You're welcome to stay overnight. Have fish with us tomorrow."

"Much obliged, but I'll be on my way." Mr. Kleinschmidt looked around the place. "McCracken. I'll have reason to remember that name."

"I wish I'd never seen Mr. Kleinschmidt," Maureen burst out, as he drove away. She put her arms around Mama. "Why did it happen? The wonderful apple is gone. Didn't mean anything. I wish I'd never found it."

Mama held her close. "Don't grieve over an apple."

Maureen felt frantic. "What shall I do?"

"Go into the kitchen and finish that applesauce." There was a catch in Mama's voice.

21.

After a hard April shower on Sunday morning, the sky cleared to a cloudless blue. Mama had packed baskets to be taken to the Wiley place and was getting ready to go to the fish fry. Maureen watched her comb her lovely brown hair. Waves fell into place with a flip of the comb and a push of her hand. In the dresser mirror, she saw Maureen. "You'll be the last one ready. Better shake a leg."

"I'm not going," Maureen announced.

Mama turned around, "Yes, you are."

"Mama, please, I don't want to go. All day long there will be a big to-do about Skeets, such a little bit of a fixing, and how she got the biggest fish ever was in Lost Creek. She didn't catch him sportsmanlike. Anybody could club a fish in a mud puddle."

Mama dusted a little powder on her nose. "Anybody

could, but she's the one who did it. So that's the difference."

"And besides Hazel will be mooning around over Mit. And he's making no headway at being nice to her. It just makes me sick." Maureen held her stomach.

"How about Sansoucies? If they come, they'll be asking about you."

"Asking about my apple, and there won't be anything to tell them. Can't I stay home, Mama?"

"No, and that's enough bellyaching out of you." Mama took a final look in the mirror and straightened things on her dresser. "You can't mope and pout here at home, put a damper on Cora's big day. It's the first chance she and Millard have had to do much for anyone. 'It's more blessed to give than to receive,' Cora says, and she's glad to give for a change. So get your duds on."

As Maureen polished her scuffed shoes, she thought of how unreasonable Mama was. The starched gingham dress she put on was too short, like all her dresses. She brushed her black hair smooth. There was no way she could push it into waves.

At the Wiley place, there was confusion inside and out. Uncle Millard and Oren shouted for the little kids to get out of the way as they carried long boards and sawhorses to make a table under the yard chinquapin tree. In the kitchen, Aunt Cora clattered stove lids to see if the cook-stove fire was right for frying. She called for Vido to come dip pieces of fish in egg batter and for Dessie to roll them in meal. Maureen was given a turner and told to watch one of the skillets on the big stove top.

She stood as far out of the way as possible. From the

192

window, she could see Skeets doing backbends like croquet hoops that all the younger children tried to imitate. She soon had a big audience. Mrs. Nolen and her husband arrived. Stackhouses came in their truck. Hazel got out wearing a blue dress that was as pretty as a ready-made one. Maureen recognized the material from the bolt of voile from Stackhouses' store. Hazel looked as if she had sent off for another sample of Tangee rouge.

When Mrs. Wiley drove up in her Durant, Grandma got out of the front seat and called Mit, who took a wooden keg covered with burlap out of the back. Grandma had brought ice cream from Beaumont. Maureen realized she would have been very discourteous to have stayed home.

The last skillet was sizzling, and Mama was setting the table when Grandma came in. "Maureen, I was looking for you. I'll spell you for a while. Go out and play with the other children."

"I don't want to, Grandma. Much obliged just the same."

Grandma studied Maureen. "You're kind of down-in-the-mouth. Now that's not like you."

"It's about my apple, the one I gave you at the fair." Maureen turned a piece of fish. "I thought it would do well to win a fair prize, but it could have been better than that. Been a new apple for the whole world. Only it's gone."

Grandma patted her shoulder. "Now stand up straight. I heard, honey. Your dad told me."

Maureen didn't try to throw back her shoulders.

"Losing the suitable compensation, that was bad enough. But I told Skeets and Oren and Vido and Dessie, everybody, that you never could tell when a wonderful thing would happen in the Saint Francois Mountains. I thought my apple would show them so for sure. Make them like Dotzero the way I do."

"It's a downright shame, Maureen. Having that nursery fellow come raised your hopes."

"I'm having trouble knowing how to be abased," Maureen admitted.

She glanced out the window and saw the Sansoucies coming. Rose was ahead, running, which wasn't easy considering she had a little brother on her hip. Suddenly Maureen felt like abounding. She gave Grandma the turner and ran out to meet Rose.

When dinner was ready, Aunt Cora lined everyone up for plates. Platters of hot fish steamed. Baskets of biscuits, bowls of browned potatoes, dark boiled greens, and pink applesauce were in place. Aunt Cora asked for a blessing on the bounty.

Uncle Millard started a speech. "We've lived like Thoreau up here. Learned what we could do without. But now the days are longer. Scratching is better, so more eggs. Spring grass is here, so more milk. That makes for good batter on this catfish, fresh, fried crisp, and not too many bones. Skeets stopped on her way home from school and picked up this fish, so we've got her to thank for this fish fry today."

"Yes, Millard, and it's getting cold." Mrs. Wiley stepped out of line and took a large piece of golden fried fish. Then everyone started filling his plate.

194

There was enough fish to go around and scraps left for Uncle Millard's cat. Mit brought the wooden keg from the shade of the porch and loosened the plug in the side to let water drain from the ice inside. He removed the damp burlap from the top and with his big hands dug into the ice beneath. Maureen sucked a sliver of salty ice. She could hardly wait for Mit to reach the can that held the sweet, firm core inside.

Ice cream was even better than Maureen had remembered. With her spoon, she scraped off small bits to form her serving into a perfect pyramid. Each bite melted in her mouth and slid down her throat. She marveled that anything could taste so delicious.

Rose brought her serving and sat on the step beside Maureen. "At the big farmhouse, they have a big white electric refrigerator now. They can have ice cream every day."

"Does it still taste like ice cream?" Maureen wondered.

After dinner, Dessie wanted to play games. Maureen thought she could keep abounding if they played some of her favorites. She jumped up and down and shrieked for prison base, wolf-over-the-ridge, red light. Dessie rejected them all as having too much running so soon after a big dinner. She wanted to play go-in-and-out-the-windows and appointed herself it.

When the song directed her to "turn to the east, turn to the west, turn to the very one that you love best," Dessie stood right in front of Melvin Stackhouse.

Maureen was glad she didn't have to be it in such a silly game. Pleased or displeased, the next game selected was worse. Everyone sat in a circle on the ground. "Look at Mit," Maureen whispered to Rose, who was next to her. "He's sitting across from Hazel as far away as he can get. That's no way to behave when she's made herself that nice dress, and she's friendly as a lost pup. Mama thinks Mit's just trying to figure out how to change and be nice to her."

Rose glanced over at Mit. "Maybe that's right, Maureen."

"Well, I think Mit has acted dumb long enough," Maureen said. "He likes her, and he ought to own up to it, stop being mule stubborn. Then he'd feel better. He needs a push in the right direction."

Skeets was chosen it and went around the circle asking players if they were pleased or displeased. Oren was displeased and requested Walter to whistle "Ain't Gonna Rain No More." Walter could barely keep his face straight enough to whistle. But he managed it and avoided a big penalty.

Maureen fidgeted, anxious for her turn. She nudged Rose and whispered to her that she thought she knew how to give Mit the needed push. When Skeets asked her the routine question of the game, Maureen announced that she was displeased.

"And what would please you better?" Skeets inquired.

"It would please me better if Mit McCracken sat by Hazel Stackhouse and told her when he's going to give her the Kewpie doll he keeps in his dresser drawer."

Maureen dodged as Mit lunged at her. "You'll have to tell her or pay a forfeit." She shouted loud enough for Uncle Millard to hear.

"Mit and Hazel, Mit and Hazel," some of the little children began to chant.

"Oh, I'll tell her," Mit said to silence the teasing. "First I'll tell her about my daffy sister, Reen Peen. She gets big ideas. Reen Peen, Reen Peen, thought she'd be the apple queen."

Others took up the chant. "Thought she'd be the apple queen. Reen Peen, Reen Peen, thought she'd be the apple queen."

"Hush up, everybody! You're not playing fair!" Maureen yelled.

"It would please me better if Maureen showed me a unicorn," Dessie said with a snicker.

"It's not your turn." Maureen tried to restore order.

"Reen Peen, thought she'd be the apple queen." Mit started again. Maureen knew she couldn't stop him. She was furious. Mit was the meanest brother anyone ever had. He couldn't stand any teasing even when it might smooth the way for him. Somehow he had turned the teasing on her.

Near tears, she fled the circle. The weighted yard gate closed with a thump behind her. She didn't slow down to look back until she was far down the lane.

A new game had started, and Walter was following her. "Mit said I should come see why you're down here poking around by yourself," Walter said, when he caught up with her.

Maureen tried to wipe her eyes on the shoulder of her dress. "As if he didn't know. Hazel better watch out for him. I don't know why anybody would like him unless she was his own sister and had to." They heard snatches of song about a little yellow basket. "Look up there, Walter. Did you ever see anything worse than Mit and Melvin stumbling over their big feet trying to skip?"

"Let's go back, Maureen," Walter pulled at her hand.

"I don't know how to go back, once I've left," Maureen admitted. "They'd all call me Reen Peen and say that dumb verse now that Mit has taught it to everybody in creation. I don't see how he could be so mean in front of Hazel and all Aunt Cora's company."

Maureen picked a dandelion and held the split, bitter-tasting stem to her tongue until it curled to the blossom. She hung dandelion curls over her ears. "How would I look with yellow hair?"

"Funny," Walter said.

She hung the curls on Walter's head. "Now you look like the new calf. The one with curly hair."

Walter brushed the curls away. "Let's go back."

"You go, Walter. There's too much hubbub there to suit me. Go see if Skeets has taught everybody how to do backbends. In case anybody should ask about me, you can tell them I've gone for a stroll by myself."

As Maureen watched him walk away, slowly at first, then faster, she wished she, too, could slip back somehow and join the fun.

Mrs. Wiley's cattle grazing near the fence stopped eating and looked curiously at Maureen. Now there were lots of calves that stayed together like children at a picnic. Their coats were cherry red, and their faces white as sheets from a school tablet.

Beside the lane, a flock of goldfinches ate dandelion

seeds. There was one brilliant indigo bunting among them. Maureen wished she could have shown it to Walter or to Rose.

Sansoucies would soon start home, for they had a long way to go. She didn't know when she would see Rose again. Maureen hadn't had near enough time to visit with her. She decided to go to the Cold Spring wagon track and wait for the Sansoucies. She'd walk partway home with Rose and have a talk with her after all.

In the Wiley pasture, she stopped to pick bunches of tart sheep sorrel and eat them—stems, leaves, flowers, and all. Against the spring grass, the cedars in the Wiley cemetery looked black as the iron fence that surrounded it. Blue blossoms studded the carpet of myrtle around the mossy headstones. Except for the oaks, the trees in McCrackens' woods were turning from pastel to many shades of green. A flock of crows circled around a tall dead tree and cawed at Maureen. She had left the singing and shouts of play far behind.

The road she came to was too well traveled to be the old wagon track that Sansoucies would follow. It must be the back road to the Wiley place on which Patsy had pulled them on Christmas Day.

Maureen crossed the road, and a blackberry patch she didn't remember soon barred her way. She circled around it and tried to save her shoes from sharp rocks. The Cold Spring track would be easier walking, but she went a long way and didn't come to it. Maureen didn't see how she could have missed the track but felt she had. She decided to return to the Wiley lane and start all over again.

22

Maureen found herself walking on a high ridge that she didn't recall. It went on and on like a dragon's backbone. The woods were denser and darker too, for rain clouds had again rolled in across the sun. As she hurried along, Maureen looked ahead, expecting limbs to clear away leaving a gray sky empty of treetops. Then she would know the back road was just ahead. But no break came in the trees.

Much as she wanted to see Rose, she decided to give up her search for the way Sansoucies would pass. She'd have to settle for getting herself straightened out and back to her own home before anyone came looking for her. She sure didn't want Skeets or any of her cousins to know that she had become confused right near the McCracken place. If Mit found out she'd done such a ridiculous thing, she'd never hear the end of it. She was not supposed to go and get herself lost.

There was no sun to help her with directions, but from the ridge she could see another rise far in the distance. Lost Creek surely flowed between them. Aunt Cora had said the Lord Himself couldn't make two hills without a hollow. She turned in the direction of the distant ridge and stumbled along over rocks and through underbrush. When she looked back to see if she had come downhill, the trees kept moving.

Maureen sat down on the soggy ground and covered her face with her arms. She listened for sounds—the farm bell, shouts from play, a train whistle, voices and footsteps of the Sansoucies in the nearby timber. All she heard were spring calls of robins and song sparrows, singing as if there were no trouble in the world. She got up and looked first one way, then the other, trying to decide which way to go. The trees spun around, so she waited and listened until they stood still. If she stayed in one place, Tisket might pick up her trail and find her.

She no longer cared about being teased for getting lost on her home ground. Now she wanted to be found. She cupped her hands around her mouth and shouted as loud as she could. An echo from the far ridge was the only response. She looked for crumbled leaves that could be a path of range stock, but there was not a trace. As she went on, she didn't try to wipe away the tears that stained her face. There was no one to see anyhow.

Abruptly she came to a road, a real road with tire tracks and a strip of grass between. There was no way to tell which way she should go on this unknown road. Maybe no one lived on it, for she couldn't hear a dog bark, a rooster crow, or a child shout at play. But all roads led someplace, so she started down this one.

Around a curve, a huge metal framework slanted across the road. Maureen came into a clearing and realized that the framework was one of four legs that supported a little house high above her. An open stairway, steep and narrow, led up to it. She knew she had come to the fire tower of Dotzero State Forest.

She had always seen it from a distance as a little box on top of a spindly scaffold. Here heavy girders held a house high above the treetops. She was amazed to find herself there, so far from where she had intended to be.

Maureen kicked at rotting leaves wet from heavy showers. The trees were leafing out. Fire season was over. No one would come to the fire tower for weeks and weeks.

Dotzero State Forest was vast. Maureen had heard Mrs. Nolen tell the eighth grade it was 30 percent of Beaumont County. She must go toward home, not deeper into the forest on the fire tower road. As she walked around the supports, she gazed up at the little house that was the same on all sides.

Then she had an encouraging idea. If she could see the top of the fire tower from home, she should be able to see home from the top of the fire tower. All she had to do was climb that steep, narrow, open stairway.

She went up fifteen steps and stopped. Remembering that Skeets climbed trees for amusement was no help.

Maureen forced herself upward. She was sure there was nothing in the little house. All the same, as she went higher and higher, she felt like an intruder, like Jack climbing his beanstalk. The house was too small for a giant, but it would be a dandy hideout for a robber or a burglar.

She didn't hold the flimsy handrail that was so high it threw her off balance. The stair turned, went up higher, turned again. She dared a downward glance at squat trees that seemed hammered into the ground. A wave of nausea warned her not to look down again.

A few more shaky steps brought her to the awful place where the steps disappeared into an opening in an overhead platform. It was far worse than the opening into the hayloft from the barn ladder. She couldn't see anything through the hole except the gray sky above.

Maureen didn't dare lean back far enough to see if there was a railing around the platform. If there was nothing to grab hold of up there, she might get dizzy, stagger, and fall from the very top of the tower. She would be found dead, and no one would ever know she'd been brave enough to climb it. They would all think she'd just stubbed her toe and hit her head on a rock.

She lowered one foot and thought it would never hit the firm support of the step below. One thing sure, she couldn't go all the way down the stairs backward. If she tried to turn around, she would miss her footing on the narrow step. There was no choice; she had to climb through the opening to the platform.

One more sickening step put her head above the platform. With her elbows on the rough boards for leverage, she pulled herself onto the narrow platform and crawled across it to the windowed house. She clung to the wall as she slowly rose on trembling legs to look into the single room. A chair was drawn up to a map-covered table in one corner. In the center of the room was a disc, big as a wagon wheel, marked into many sections. With windows on all sides, the room was light, even on a cloudy day.

Maureen released her embrace of the wall long enough to turn around. She was relieved to see a sturdy railing around the platform. Still, there was a chance of falling down the stair opening, so she flattened herself against the tower room. She caught her breath as she looked over the leafing treetops to the near hills and the far blue ridges. Never before had she seen the full beauty of the Saint Francois Mountains, where she had lived all her life.

She gained courage to look down and see the road she had come on disappear in the timber. It might go halfway to Beaumont. She was glad she had not followed it. Keeping her back to the tower room and her arms spread out to feel its support, Maureen slowly moved around it for another wondrous view of wooded hills.

Another turn around the building brought sights that lifted her burden of dread and made her light-headed with joy. From such a height, things looked flattened and a little strange, but she knew what they were. A little yellow box was Dotzero depot. The long, low building was Stackhouses' store and the United States Post

Office. She could see the worn playground around the school. A toy train, like one she had seen in a Beaumont store window, moved along a tiny straight track. Lost Creek looped and turned.

Without thinking, Maureen moved to the railing on the fourth side for the best sight of all. Skeets was right. Things did look different from high places. The toy train, which must be Number 32, crossed the high trestle over Lost Creek. Brown as March, McCrackens' bottom field stood out from the surrounding April green. The Johnson grass wasn't sprouting. A ghost must have killed it, just as she had predicted to Walter. The three dormer windows of her own house showed plainly. Hanging from the yard oak, the tire swing looked like a rubber band. Lush circles of darker green in the orchard showed where the brush piles had been and where fescue now thrived.

Patsy was lying down in the pasture adjoining the orchard and barn lot. Eating was a steady job for Molly, but she had stopped grazing to look at something that moved near Patsy. At first, Maureen thought they were deer, but according to Mrs. Nolen deer had been gone from Beaumont County since the late nineteenth century. They were too big for dogs, so they might be two of Mrs. Wiley's calves that had escaped from her pasture when company left the gates open. But they were dark brown, not red.

Maureen gripped the railing in excitement. Patsy had a colt! She had two! Twins! Patsy certainly had been looking fat, but she thought that was from good spring pasture. No one had told her a foal was expected. Her family must think she was a bigger baby than Yvonne. But now she was first to know Patsy had twins. From her high perch, she'd figure the right direction to go, get down, and tell everybody.

A dark, straight line parting the timber showed the fire tower road leading out of the forest and joining the back road to the Wiley place just beyond the lane gate. The low Wiley house was plain as day, but she wasn't sure there was anyone in the yard. Maybe the fish fry was over. She looked to see if her family was going home across the fields.

At the edge of McCrackens' woods near the ridge field, something white caught her eye. It looked like a tree branch in bloom. But it couldn't be wild plum. That had gone by. Dogwood was still to come. Yellow green of sassafras was on one side of the white branch and the still-bare honey locust on the other. It was right where she had cut Epitome out of the fence. A branch of her wild apple had lived and now bloomed! She was sure of it.

Her heart thumped as she took the first fearful step off the platform down to the stair. She went faster with each step that brought her closer to the ground. Near the bottom, she took the steps two at a time the way she did the stairs at home, and she hit the ground running.

As she raced along the fire tower road, she watched like a hunting hawk for the back road turnoff. There was no time to get lost again.

23

Skeets, darting around the chinquapin tree as if she were tethered to it, was the only one to be seen at Uncle Millard's. Maureen wanted to shout to bring everyone from the house, but she was so breathless from running that she slumped down beside the tree. "Get everybody so's I can tell them all," she panted to Skeets.

"Come in free. All that's out, come in free," Skeets called, and left her base unguarded to go inside. Children popped out of hiding and came from all directions to touch the base tree of the I spy game. Maureen crawled aside to avoid being trampled.

Of the gang that rushed out of the house, Mama was first to reach Maureen. She felt her arms and shoulders as if checking for broken bones. "Maureen! What is it? Tell us!"

Mit looked at her tangled hair, dirty face, torn dress, what was left of her shoes. "Man alive, do you look awful!"

Maureen tried to smooth her hair. "You'd look awful too if you'd been where I've been."

"Where's that, Maureen? Where on earth have you been?" Mama asked. "Mrs. Wiley was looking for you."

"I've been everywhere." Maureen waved her arm in a circle. She looked around the group. "Have Sansoucies gone?"

"Long time ago," Skeets answered.

"I missed them more ways than one." Maureen sighed. "But I can write Rose a letter or else call them on the telephone and tell them."

Mama took Maureen by the shoulders. "Tell them what? Are you hurt, Maureen? Did you fall. What is it?"

"Nope, not a bit hurt, not snakebit, or anything." Maureen was enjoying all the attention.

Mrs. Wiley stooped down to peer sharply at her. "Are my cattle all right? Epitome? All the calves?"

"Oh, sure, Mrs. Wiley, prettiest herd in Beaumont County, like you say."

Aunt Cora looked around the landscape and sniffed. "Anything afire?"

Maureen shook her head. "I don't think so. First I saw her lying on the ground, and I thought—"

"Saw who lying on the ground?" Mit questioned.

"Patsy."

"Oh, Cleve," Mama wailed. "Patsy's time came! We were afraid the colt would be dead. I wish you could have been spared that sight, Maureen."

"What about Patsy?" Mit yelled.

Walter sat down beside Maureen. "Did Patsy live all winter and die in the spring?"

Maureen took a deep breath. "I'm trying to tell you."

"Spit it out, Maureen," Mit demanded.

"I saw her lying down, and then I saw Molly looking at these things, dogs or deer or something. Couldn't tell for sure from where I was." Maureen took her time. "You wouldn't believe it, but I'm just about sure something has happened on the McCracken place that never happened before. Hardly ever happens."

Mit paced with impatience "What?"

"Patsy didn't have a colt. She had two! Twins."

"Alive? Not both alive, are they?" Dad's voice was anxious.

"Well, they were standing up, but, of course, I wasn't too close."

Mit started laughing and jumping around like a little kid on Christmas morning. "I knew it was about time. I'm taking off, got to see about this." He grabbed Hazel's hand. "You can come too if you want to."

"How come Mit knew about it and I didn't?" Maureen demanded. "Nobody bothered to tell me. Here I thought her belly was sagging because she's so swaybacked. When I know something, I tell people. Try to make things interesting. Why didn't anybody let me in on the big news?"

Dad held out his hand to help Maureen to her feet. "It was chancy, Maureen. We didn't expect Patsy to go full time and have a live colt, let alone two. An old mare like Patsy usually drops a dead colt. We were trying to save you more disappointment. You'd had enough losing your good wild apple."

"My apple tree! Even before I go see those twins, I'm having a closer look at it. At first, I thought it couldn't be true. Must be a little strip of cambium layer was left on that broken limb and the rabbits didn't nibble quite through it. Because there it is, right up at the edge of McCrackens' woods."

"What, Maureen?" Walter asked. "What's up there?"

"Apple blossoms on one last broken limb of our apple tree," Maureen announced.

A pained look came over Dad's face. "Are you sure, Maureen?"

"It seemed so from where I was. And something else. Everything is going green except our bottom field. It's brown and empty as last year's bird's nest. Not a blade of Johnson grass showing, so we can raise corn there again this year. Come on, everybody, let's go see the apple tree." Maureen was ready to start, but Mama held her back.

She tied Maureen's sash and tried to smooth her dress. "Just a minute, hon. We were all wondering where you were. Mrs. Wiley has something to say to you."

Mrs. Wiley stood directly in front of Maureen as if ready to start a ceremony. She held a flat metal box and a large tablet of paper. "Now, Maureen, I've kept in mind that you were uncommon levelheaded in preventing serious injury to Epitome of Lower Upson. I paid a scandalous price for him on the strength of his pedigree alone. Before I had added expense of a reward for you, I wanted to see the quality of the calves he sired. They're true to the

210

breed, champions all. So I have this for you." She handed Maureen the box and tablet. "I never put out cash for anything like it before. I got it from Sears, the best money can buy. Now I would have selected something far more practical. But Skeets, the little wiry one, told me this would please you. She thought so because you admired Will Wiley's old painting so much."

Maureen opened the box and marveled at the rows of little tubes marked *Watercolor, Artists' Quality*. Three different-sized brushes nested between the rows of tubes that were banded in every color. The wide lid was indented into sections.

Mama nudged Maureen. "Oh, thank you, Mrs. Wiley. I never thought I'd ever have anything like this. Surprised me so, I almost forgot my manners."

As Maureen showed her gift she was careful not to let the little kids squeeze the tubes of paint or smear the white pebbly paper of the tablet. Before all had admired the watercolor set, Dessie yelled that she would beat everybody to McCrackens' to see the twin colts. The children took off across the fields like a pack of hounds. Some of the grown-ups followed on foot. Others piled into their cars to drive. Everyone was going except Dad.

Maureen latched the box lid with its pressure catches. "Let's go look at my tree, Dad. That's what I want to see most."

Despite all her amazing news, Dad still looked troubled. "We'd better go with the rest and make sure Patsy isn't disturbed by too many too close to her babies. Then I'll swing around by the bottom field. I've had my eye on that too. Something there has me bested. We'll get to your apple tree later."

Maureen chanted to herself "How to be abated and how to abound." On "abound," she took long leaps and soon caught up with the rest.

At McCrackens' pasture, folks did their best to keep their distance and their voices low in the excitement of seeing twin colts for the first time. Patsy was up and looked proudly at her identical colts as they wobbled on their long legs to nurse from her udder, black and leathery as a pocketbook.

Mit pranced around as if he wanted to whoop and holler. In a low voice, he kept repeating, "I did it. I did it. I got us a team of mules."

He had neglected to comb his hair, but he had stopped to pick up something at the house. Bright against her blue dress were the purple feathers of the Kewpie doll that Hazel cradled in arms. She had gotten rid of her gum and was smiling as smugly as the Kewpie.

Mit drew Maureen aside. "You were right. I don't know how you knew, but Patsy *is* a wonder horse. That's what you told me after Dad made me feel like a whipped dog when I brought her home. I sure didn't know I'd get us the mules we need this way. I guess I showed folks that Mit McCracken could manage for a team."

Maureen nodded toward Hazel. "You showed everybody."

"Whatever you say, Maureen. You might even be the apple queen." Mit dodged as if expecting blows from Maureen. She felt more like hugging him. A big brother

212

was strange. He could make a person feel madder or gladder than almost anyone else.

Maureen saw Walter off by himself swaying near the top of the fence. Clutching her paint set and tablet, she went to steady him. "Tomorrow, when it's quieter, nobody strange to Patsy around, we'll go in and pet them, Walter."

"They aren't unicorns, Maureen. I can tell from here. They don't have red hoofs."

"Well, of course not. You can't expect Patsy to do everything. She did well to have two mule colts."

Walter climbed down from the fence. "Why?"

"Because she's a mare, and Mrs. Wiley's jack is the father. It's a bigger mystery than why she had a unicorn once. Don't you ask Mama or Dad or Mit about it because they won't tell you one thing, and you'll be in trouble besides for asking. Do you know what percent chance there was for an old mare like Patsy to have a colt?"

Walter shook his head.

"About 10 percent," Maureen said knowingly. "And the chance of her having twin colts, well that's about 5 percent. The chance of them both being born alive and walking around right this minute is about this much." Maureen jabbed for a point and drew figures in the air. "Zero-decimal point-five percent. That means one-half of 1 percent. It beats a unicorn for chances and for work stock too. Unicorns aren't much account for that. Not dependable."

"Can't you tell me some way besides percent? We don't have that in third grade."

"You're going to have it, and you might as well listen

to the upper grades and learn ahead the way I do," Maureen advised.

"I'm real glad you found a way to get back to the fish fry," Walter said.

"Me too. It was kind of roundabout."

Walter started to chase about Boots, Buddy, and Mertie in a game of tag. He stopped and hung back waiting for Maureen. She motioned him away. "Just go ahead. Go on with them. Take turns in the tire swing."

Walter looked sad. "Are you mad at me?"

"No, not mad at anybody. I know I can't have you forever asking me questions and tagging after me." Walter smiled so broadly that his eyes closed to sparkling slits. Then he turned and ran with his cousins down the slope from the pasture.

Maureen watched the flow of visitors go down the hill. They would spread the news of the twin colts. Mrs. Wiley and Grandma would see that it was known in Beaumont. She didn't see Dad or Uncle Millard, but she knew they were somewhere on the place.

Maureen rubbed at finger marks on her paint box. Ever since she'd had an idea for using it, she felt she had finally got rid of the green-eyed monster.

On McCrackens' porch, Aunt Cora eased down into the big rocker. "This is one evening I won't have to cook supper. We'll wait here for Millard. He must have had too much company and gone off on one of his Thoreau rambles."

Maureen put her paint set on the far end of the porch out of the way of little children and went to the kitchen for a cup of water. When she came out, Mama was talking to Aunt Cora. "Events of the day will soon be known far and wide. Sterling Stackhouse won't have much to say, though. He had no notion Patsy was due for a colt, let alone two, when he bartered her for Mit's work. It makes up a little for the other—" Mama stopped when she noticed Maureen.

"Other what?" Maureen asked.

"Later, Maureen. Now what are you up to with that water?" Mama looked to make sure the cup was cracked.

"Skeets is going to teach me how to use my new paints," Maureen announced. "First lesson now, while I'm waiting for Dad to go with me up to my tree. I don't want to barge around by myself anymore today. Over here, Skeets, where the kids won't kick over the water."

Skeets looked at the pristine paper and paints. "Are you sure you want me to use your brand-new stuff?"

"Yes, I thought about it. I'd waste more trying to learn how to use it than you will showing me. You know how from city school. I believe it now. So if I didn't ask you, I'd be biting off my nose to spite my face."

Skeets squeezed tiny mounts of color into the pans of the lid. She wet the large brush. "I like to do this so much it gives me goose bumps." She looked toward the barn lot where Mit was leading Patsy, followed by her colts. "There are plenty of things around to make pictures of. At first, I didn't see them, but I do now." She made a puddle of blue in the lid, dipped in her brush, and flowed a blue sky across the paper. "Now we'll have to wait a little until it dries."

"We'll trade off lessons," Maureen said. "As soon as Lost Creek warms up, I'll help you learn to swim. You know, when you lambasted Old Whisker, you waded in, and all you had to do was—*slurp*—step out of your shoes. But sometime you might wade into something too deep. Step into a hole. Around here, you ought to know how to swim. It's fun besides."

With a little more paint and a little less water, Skeets made the Saint Francois Mountains darker than the sky. A touch of blue, then yellow made a pool of green that became spring grass on the paper. Slaps of the brush became trees.

Skeets made light-brown tree trunks. "Now here's a trick." She soaked the brush with darker brown and flicked it down one side of the trunks to make them look round. The barn she blocked in became real as she darkened one side and half the roof. "Sunlight does that," she said, as if she had nothing to do with the effect. She mixed a dark color and put it over the lovely green at one side of the barn, as if she meant to ruin the whole picture. But the dark mass formed a shadow.

"I can walk around that barn." Maureen was fascinated.

Skeets hooked her long hair back of her ears and bent over the painting. "I'll put in Patsy. I like to do animals." Skeets drew with the smallest brush, then painted Patsy's sorrel coat lighter on her back, dark under her belly, so that Patsy too looked real. Carefully she painted the spindly legged colts.

Maureen's fingers itched to hold the brush. "I can do it. Today I'd believe anything. I thought you had to be born with the talent to make pictures, but maybe not. You can learn. I think, though, you have to be born *wanting* to make pictures."

Skeets darkened the foliage on one side of the trees. "You'll slop around for a while the way I'll splash around learning to swim. I'm glad you let me use these. I want to learn a lot more too."

Then Skeets did an odd thing. She painted a little horn on the head of each colt.

"They aren't unciorns, Skeets, just mules."

"Well, when you're an artist, you can have them be whatever you want." Skeets jumped up as if she could not be still another minute and ran to the tire swing.

Everyone was admiring the painting when Dad came up from the bottom field. "Now that's a real keepsake of the big day at the McCracken place. Here's something remarkable too." He showed them a shriveled root. "What do you think of this?"

Mama took it from him and sniffed it. "I'd say it's rotten."

"That's a Johnson grass tuber that won't ever sprout. We've got a field of it," Dad said.

"Thanks be!" Mama tossed the root away. "Good riddance. What killed it?"

"Death due to drowning," Dad declared. "You know high water rampaged over the field. Then it calmed down and just stood there stagnant for a few days. Finally it went down so gradually it caught Old Whisker napping. The water smothered out and rotted the Johnson grass roots. By planting time in a few weeks, Patsy will be up to

217

a little plowing. We can get in a crop of corn for our increased stock."

"That's just what Maureen said would happen. Something like that," Walter said.

"On that order." Maureen took Dad's hand. "Now are you ready to go to the apple tree? We'd better get up there before dark."

Dad sat down on the porch steps. "Maureen, I'd rather take a beating than tell you what I must. I know you've had renewed hopes for that apple. You helped the rest of us keep up hopes too during a corn-bread winter. I figure you helped us get a just price for our hogs. Talked up at the right time. Cora says you came up with something that helped her get work.

"But we got to where something more had to be done, especially after I realized Patsy was going to have a colt— just one, I figured. First I thought she was bloated and was mighty surprised to feel movement. There was little chance she'd have a live colt at the end of the term. But, even so, we wanted her to have a chance, get the grain and hay needed. That meant cash. We had a big store bill that had to be settled. So the long and short of it is that McCrackens' woods don't belong to us now. I sold it to Sterling Stackhouse."

"It's ours. It's part of the McCracken place," Maureen insisted. "Stackhouses have almost as much land as Mrs. Wiley."

Aunt Cora quoted, "For unto every one that hath shall be given, and he shall have abundance; but from him that hath not shall be taken away even that which he hath."

218

"That's not fair." Maureen was near tears.

"Careful, Maureen, that's Scripture," Mama cautioned. "Anyhow, it wasn't given. Sterling Stackhouse paid for it fair and square. He always did want a good woodlot."

Aunt Cora got up from her chair. "I guess Millard's home already, and we'd better get there while it's still light. Vido, round everybody up."

The place was very quiet after all the cousins had gone. Maureen sat on the porch holding the paint set hard against her chest, hoping the hardness of it would help her get over the odd empty feeling she had. Dad was silent and might stay so for a long time.

Someone came from the ridge field toward the house. Although it was dusk, Maureen could tell by the stoop of the shoulders that it was Uncle Millard.

"I had to go see about Maureen's posies." Uncle Millard sat down on the bottom step. "I've been doing some line-of-sight surveying. She's right. One branch with two scions is alive on the hanging limb. And when that limb came down, it fell right across the property line onto your land, Cleve. You know the law: Anything over the line belongs to you."

"Are you sure it fell over the line?" Dad spoke loudly to Uncle Millard.

"I helped run the line when Stackhouse sent the surveyor to make sure he got every foot he paid for."

Dad nodded. "The day we had the fire in the orchard."

"So I took the sight from the corner of the Wiley cemetery iron-fence corner, and that limb is yours. Stackhouse knows about the nursery offer, but you're in the clear to make your nursery stock cutting. I'll swear to it if needs be. I'd better get home and tell the rest about Maureen's apple."

Maureen jumped up. "Now that's what I call a smidgen!"

"My, what a day!" Mama hugged Maureen. "I started out wondering if we'd have enough fish to go around."

Dad slapped his leg. "If we'd had five biscuits and two little fish, we would have had plenty the way things are happening here."

They all followed Mama inside where she lit the lamp and got out her tablet to write to Lyman Kleinschmidt at Knocker Nursery.

Maureen thought about the suitable compensation. "Will we be rich?"

"A mite more comfortable, not so pinched, eased a little." Dad's eyes twinkled. "Of course, according to Millard and Thoreau, we've always been rich."

Mama started to write. "I think we should give our name for the apple. Maureen ought to have the honor. She was bound and determined that apple would amount to something."

Maureen recalled that Mr. Kleinschmidt had wished he had remembered their name. She thought too of how the apple had cracked with crispness when she took her first bite. "McCracken! I want it named McCracken," she announced.

"Fair enough." Mama dipped her pen. Her handwriting was as pretty as Mrs. Nolen's.

"Walter, don't you ever forget you were with me when

we found that tree," Maureen said, "and you watch out so you don't miss wonderful things."

"I will," he promised.

"I like to think of how we'll be abounding—Uncle Millard's family and Grandma and all of us." Maureen looked thoughtful. "Mostly, though, I like to imagine somebody in a store pointing to big red apples and saying, 'I'll take a peck of those McCrackens. They're the best.'"

ABOUT THE AUTHOR

Marian Potter was born in Blackwell, Missouri, fifty miles south of Saint Louis. After attending public school in DeSoto, Missouri, she went to the University of Missouri at Columbia, where she graduated with a degree in journalism. Her professional writing experience is very diverse, including staff and free-lance work in broadcasting, advertising, industry, and journalism. In addition, Ms. Potter is the author of several books for children.

A mother of three, and grandmother of two, Marian Potter now lives with her husband in Warren, Pennsylvania.